MORE GHOST STORIES of SHIMLA HILLS

Minakshi Chaudhry, an author and former journalist, lives in Shimla with her husband. She is a keen observer of people, culture, lifestyles, and loves trekking and travelling.

Minakshi has authored several books—*Sunshine: My Encounter with Cancer, Love Stories of Shimla Hills, Whispering Deodars: Writings from Shimla Hills, Destination Himachal: 132 Offbeat and 12 Popular Getaways, Ghost Stories of Shimla Hills, 65 Treks and Over 100 Destinations: A Guide to Trekking in Himachal,* and *Exploring Pangi Himalaya: A World Beyond Civilization.*

She is currently working on her next book and can be contacted at minakshi_kanwar@yahoo.com

MINAKSHI CHAUDHRY

RUPA

First published in 2012 by
Rupa Publications India Pvt. Ltd.
7/16, Ansari Road, Daryaganj,
New Delhi 110 002

Sales Centres:

Allahabad Bengaluru Chennai
Hyderabad Jaipur Kathmandu
Kolkata Mumbai

10 9 8 7 6 5 4 3 2 1

Printed and bound in India by
Nutech Photolithographers
B-240, Okhla Industrial Area, Phase-I,
New Delhi-110 020

To

The ghosts, spirits and chudails of Shimla Hills.

Thank you for bringing more zing into our lives!

Contents

Preface

I do believe in ghosts—these tales are what I *really* heard and I fear encountering the supernatural. This fear is enhanced on dark moonless nights, especially when I am alone on a lonely stretch or when the mist envelops hills and valleys and something howls from the faraway jungle... But I must also tell another truth: I haven't met a ghost, so far.

Shimla is the perfect place for these supernatural beings to survive the onslaught of modern times. The plot is set for unfolding many more scary and real ghostly tales. Ghosts prefer the thick, dark groves; murky alleys and lonely spots; uninhabited forested paths; *bowlis* (natural water points) and springs. They love the hills. And the queen of hills, Shimla, has so many nooks, corners, thickets and springs...even today!

These stories also tell us about the cultural and religious life of hill people. Generations of Shimlaites grew up hearing stories about bhoots and chudails. These tales based on 'facts' and 'experiences' shared by people, have been narrated in a fictionalized way.

When I started working on this second collection I was amazed by the response I got. The surprised look that I got from people when I had wandered in and around Shimla in 2003, collecting tales for *Ghost Stories of Shimla Hills* was gone. It was no longer a frustrating or embarrassing experience. This time no one said to me: 'ghosts in this age?'

I met so many people who had not only enjoyed the book but who even expressed their disappointment that I had not included the 'real tale' they knew or that a popular story from their area was left out. They wanted me to include that in the second volume.

Initially, I made light of this idea but soon I realized that there was a huge demand for new stories. So tentatively, I set off; a bit hesitant and cautious. But I was in for a pleasant surprise. Searching for ghosts was so 'normal'! So many young and old people shared their experiences in a casual and matter-of-fact manner, that I felt a strange tingling.

Another interesting thing is that so many ghost stories related not to the bygone days and there is no 'once-upon-a-time' thing. These are present-day tales. Surprised?

I have collected innumerable tales, so, my dear friends, we may meet again with another book.

Join me for an exciting reading.

January 2012

Minakshi Chaudhry
Shimla

Sister Shanti and the English Nurse

Sister Kamla looked out of her hostel window. It had been snowing since the last three days in Shimla, slow and steady. A white carpet stretched endlessly where once stood the ground, flower beds and the benches. It all looked pure and beautiful.

It was the first time she had seen snow. She had come back today after a three-day leave. She had walked ten kilometres from Jutogh as no buses were plying due to heavy snowfall. She was a student nurse and belonged to Bilaspur district.

Sister Kamla was dead tired after the arduous walk and wanted to sleep for twenty-four hours but this was not possible. Her shift started at 8 o'clock in the night.

Moreover, there were so many errands to be completed before rushing to the hospital—ironing her dress, cleaning her shoes, taking a bath and having dinner. At about ten minutes to eight she reached the hospital—an old rickety building popularly known as Snowdon.

The sister's duty room was part of the male ward. The male ward was divided into two, like a stage you climbed a few steps to reach the second part where the nursing station was situated. From the station you could see all the beds in the male ward below. The dead house was at the back. Common bathrooms were near the dead house. The flooring was wooden and the building had a lot of zigzag entrances and exits with so many doors, small and big rooms. Nurses called it a bhoot-bangla jokingly.

Sister Kamla sighed with relief to find that Ward Sister Ursem was nowhere in sight. Everyone was really scared of her; if there was just a small wrinkle on the dress the ward sister would take your class as if you had committed a murder! If you were not alert enough to respond immediately to a patient's call she would reprimand you so severely in front of everyone that the next time even if a patient did not call, you would be there! She was very particular with everything—insisting on the proper way to hold and apply an injection, inserting cannula for intravenous therapy, filling out the treatment chart, measuring the fluid bags and administering medicines. A small mistake, and she made you feel like dirt. Everything had to be perfect and as per the book.

Sister Kamla knew Ward Sister Ursem was somewhere in the building and she was on duty till ten o'clock. So there wasn't any scope for carelessness. She would suddenly appear from nowhere just when you had committed a mistake.

Two student nurses were on duty that night, both senior to Sister Kamla. Then there was a resident doctor. She must do everything right till Ward Sister Ursem left and then possibly she would be able to catch a few hours of sleep. During winters there were not many patients so the student nurses took turns to nap for two to three hours.

She went through the case files, checked the prescription changes and flipped through the diet charts and case histories. There were forty patients in all with five of them critically ill, who had to be checked regularly in the night. Nearly half of the patients were on IV-fluids so the bottles had to be changed. Normally, the nurses started the last bottle around midnight at a slower infusion rate so that the fluid could go on till seven in the morning when the next shift was about to start.

Sister Kamla did the needful and noted all important observations in the file. It was quiet in the ward. As Sister Kamla flipped through the files, she heard footsteps on the wooden stairs. Someone was coming, probably Ward

Sister Ursem. As the sound came nearer, she recognized Sister Ursem's quick steps. She stood up from the chair, in attention, scared of what she might ask her—and for God's sake, where were the other nurses?

Sister Ursem entered the ward, did not utter a single word or even nod at Sister Kamla's greetings, and started the round as Sister Kamla tagged along with the treatment charts and files. She was in the ward for about fifteen long minutes, and then left.

Phew! Thank God, the lady Hitler did not say anything nasty, thought Sister Kamla. She was pleased that for the first time she had handled the ward sister alone during the round and everything had gone well, though she was surprised Sister Ursem hadn't uttered even a word to the patients or to her. This was unlike her. She hadn't even once glanced at Sister Kamla during the entire round.

A few minutes later the other two sisters came into the ward. She told them about Sister Ursem's round. They were white with fear and were quite disturbed. They were sure to be reprimanded the next day for being late. But they were not really late. They were checking the medicines in the store and bringing in the supplies for the night. How the heck did they know that the sister would come for the round at 8.30 p.m.! The time for night rounds was usually after nine o'clock.

The next couple of hours passed smoothly, Sister Kamla took the first turn to sleep from eleven o'clock to two o'clock. When she woke up, her companion sister was feeling unwell; she had fever so both her seniors went off to sleep and Sister Kamla was left alone. Not much was left to be done, though; one glucose bottle had to be changed, only one patient had to be given an injection and she had to take another patient's temperature. That was all.

However, half an hour later, Sister Kamla began to feel drowsy. For a few minutes she fought with sleep, but losing the battle she decided to lean her head on the table only to rest but dozed off. Suddenly she woke up with a start; she had been slapped hard on the cheek by someone. She was terrified, she looked at the watch, it was three o'clock. She started screaming uncontrollably. The other two sisters came running, patients woke up and some of them who could move from their beds started looking for the intruder.

For the next few moments there was chaos. Sister Kamla's cheek hurt; in fact there was a clear imprint of a hand on her cheek, so hard had she been hit. No one was found, her attacker should have been caught because she had screamed immediately when she was assaulted. In the midst of this chaos Sister Kamla remembered her patients—temperature was to be checked, injection needed to be given and the glucose bottle had to be changed. She uttered a cry of anguish and hurried to do the needful. A few moments later she was found unconscious in a heap near the patient whose glucose bottle she had to change.

Sister Kamla was discharged from the hospital a day later. She went on a two-week leave to recuperate from acute stress. No one knew what was wrong with her, she had stopped talking and answered no questions. Two weeks later a request for extension of leave was forwarded to the hospital administration by Sister Kamla's father. It was then that Ward Sister Ursem decided to meet the young student and travelled to her hometown in Bilaspur. On reaching her house she told her family members to leave them alone.

Sister Ursem felt sorry for the girl, whose pallor was as white as chalk. The truth had to be told to her and she had conveyed it to some other nurses as well just as she herself had been told by her seniors.

Student Nurse Kamla had buried what had happened deep inside her, but when she saw Sister Ursem all the horror came back. She started trembling and wept like a small child. Sister Ursem let her cry to her heart's content and when the sobs subsided she said softly, 'I know what passed that night. It wasn't your fault, though in a way it *was* your fault.' Kamla was speechless, she just shook her head; how could Ward Sister Ursem know what had transpired.

'I know, I know, child. This is related to Sister Shanti.'

'Sister Shanti?' mumbled the young student. Was Sister Shanti a senior nurse she couldn't recall from the three-month training she had undergone at the hospital.

'Yes, Sister Shanti.' It is difficult to explain about Sister Shanti, thought Sister Ursem.

'No, no. I don't know any Sister Shanti...who is she?'

'I'll tell you who she is, just calm down.'

Was Sister Ursem crazy? What had this got to do with Sister Shanti, thought the girl. 'You don't know, after you left...' started Kamla, still trembling.

'Oh dear child, calm down. I had left in the evening that day. My younger sister had slipped in the snow and broken her ankle, I was with her all the time.'

What was Sister Ursem saying? Did she not remember that *she* had come on the round. In fact, she had come an hour earlier than her usual time and Kamla had taken her around and updated her about all the patients? 'No, no, after the round...' she started again.

'It was not me but Sister Shanti who...'

'What are you saying? I don't know any Shanti, it was...'

'Oh, listen to me. Sister Shanti transforms herself into whoever she wants to be.'

'Transforms?' mumbled Kamla. What does she mean?

'Yes, calm down first and then I will tell you everything. No one knows in which year Sister Shanti had worked in the hospital but she was a dedicated nurse—someone who loved her job and took great care of her patients. Then something happened to her, no one knows what, but she died very young. And since then...well, her spirit appears and disappears on its own will. But it always makes an appearance when the patients need help, or when the nurse on duty is not doing her work.'

'You mean...' Sister Kamla was too astonished to react.

'Yes, the slap you got, the injection, the bottle, the temperature, all was done by Sister Shanti's spirit because you did not do it,' said Ursem gently.

Sister Kamla was quiet.

'And about the round that I could not make that day—I had informed the resident doctor on duty, who had assured me that there would be no problem and he would take care of everything. Moreover, there were no serious patients. But for Sister Shanti this wasn't so...' Sister Ursem didn't complete her sentence. Student Nurse Kamla also chose to keep silent.

'There is nothing to be afraid of, she is a guiding spirit and has always come to help her patients in need,' said Sister Ursem finally.

The young sister nodded in comprehension. She had understood the mystery now, and her heart brimmed with love and respect for the spirit and her dedication. Kamla too wanted to be like Sister Shanti. She was their teacher and there was no need to be afraid of her, but sisters like Kamla better do their duty with sincerity!

She went back to the hospital along with the ward sister to continue her training.

☙

Nurse Raksha sat in the sister's duty room in the all-woman hospital. For months, she was in a dilemma and wanted to know the truth. She had heard about the ghost of the English nurse, who would come to check on the newborns. Nurse Raksha was desperate to see the spirit, the guiding angel who took care of the babies and ensured that no harm came to them. Whenever a newborn needed immediate help and no doctor or nurse was around, the spirit would move in and out of the ward to make sure that a nurse noticed her and rushed to take care of the sick child.

She had heard about the English nurse's spirit from other nurses and quite recently, from a junior colleague. This junior sister had had a hysterical breakdown and had to be treated for three days before she was ready to take up her duties again; that too on the assurance that she would not be given night duty in the hospital until she had recovered fully!

The unsuspecting junior sister had no idea about this spirit when it chanced upon her. At one o'clock in the night, while the ward sister was in the special ward and two other nurses were in the labour room assisting in a delivery, she sat alone in the nurses' duty room trying to fight sleep when she looked out of the window and saw an English woman.

What a surprise! The lady was wearing a nurse's dress, not the salwar-kameez they wore but a frock with a belt, long white socks and black shoes and a different white-coloured, starched headgear—a nightingale cap. She had seen this type of dress only in magazines.

She was astonished that an English nurse was walking around the children's ward and then entering it. Speechless, she sat there mulling over what the English nurse was doing there in the middle of the night. Probably she had not seen her well, maybe it was a lady from upper Shimla. Then she saw the English woman coming out of the ward and then entering it again. This time she saw her more clearly: no, it was no Indian woman or a paharan but an English lady for sure. Her dress was so different from theirs—it was the old-fashioned English dress that nurses wore in the movies.

She was spellbound—what in hell's name was this lady doing here, when to her sheer disbelief she saw her entering the children's ward *again,* though she had not seen her coming out! Something was definitely wrong, she couldn't pinpoint it, but now she was alert. Who was this lady? How had she entered this part of the hospital when the inner gate always remained closed at night? How would she exit?

She was frantically trying to get an answer to all these questions when the lady came out of the ward again. An unknown hair-raising dread besieged her. Suddenly she realized that this was no woman, this was something unnatural...she was from another world.

Moreover, the lady was not walking but gliding, and the speed at which she was entering and coming out of the ward—no human could do that. Her mouth went dry with fear and her body trembled, maybe she should shout, ask for help, someone will definitely hear her—the chowkidar, the nurses or the patients.

She was scolding herself for being such a coward when, to her horror, the thing came again, gliding, crossing the windows and entering the children's ward. She had never felt such strange fear; she was whimpering. What was this thing doing to the babies inside the ward, she thought helplessly. This made her get up and move towards the door of the sister's room. Her legs could hardly hold her as she clutched the door frame for support, and then the ghost came out of the ward and started gliding towards her!

She closed her eyes and screamed as loud as her lungs would allow her, and did not stop screaming till the entire hospital staff came running towards her. Only then did she open her eyes and whispered incoherently while pointing towards the children's ward. The nurses left her there and ran into the ward.

They saved the lives of two small babies: one had almost choked herself with the bed sheet and in another case, the IV-fluid bottle had turned pink since the needle, having blocked the blood due to back pressure, had begun flowing into the bottle. Both the mothers were asleep, unaware of the calamity waiting to strike their children. That night there were just four children in the ward. The other two were fine with their mothers sleeping peacefully beside them.

Had the spirit not come and gone repeatedly, the nurse would not have been able to save the children; 'it' wanted to be noticed so the children could be saved. This English nurse was the guiding angel of the children's ward and it was her whom Sister Raksha wanted to see. Nothing happened that night and for several other nights while Sister Raksha watched alertly.

But then, how could something happen, Sister Raksha took care of babies in her ward so sincerely that there was no need for the ghost of the English nurse to come and intervene!

Torture Cell of the Gaiety

Is Gaiety Theatre really haunted?

Anil stopped in the middle of his thoughts while writing his talk on 'Theatre in Imperial Shimla with special reference to Gaiety Theatre', to be delivered in a seminar on World Theatre Day. Anil had a doctorate on the subject of British Theatre in Imperial India. Though he would deliver his talk on the topic, in his heart he wanted to talk about the supernatural tale associated with the Gaiety.

Anil remembered the story narrated to him by Amrit Lal on a cold winter night in December. It was a grisly and horrendous tale.

'I was a reckless and fearless boy,' the old man had begun with a smile, 'but such attitude lands you in trouble many times. As a small child I had gone to stay with my uncle for a few days in Shimla, where he worked as a cobbler. He also repaired shoes of the English people, so he got good money. Soon my uncle was fed up with my naughty pranks and asked me to return to the village...'

As the story continued, Anil was stupefied by what he heard.

'When will you go back?' his uncle asked.

'I don't know, maybe today or tomorrow. I still want to see the road with all the big shops where the English mems buy things from,' Amrit Lal said innocently.

Mathu Ram put down the shoe he was working on. He felt both anger and pity for the boy. How many times had he explained to him that it was not possible to look at sahibs and memsahibs from close quarters, that too at the Mall!

'You should understand that Mall Road is only for gora sahibs and the rich, royal Hindustanis,' he explained patiently.

'But I want to go there,' Amrit replied obstinately.

Exasperated, his uncle caught hold of the young man's shoulders and pressed the blades hard as he said, 'Won't you listen to what I have been telling you for the past one week? Mall Road is not a place for poor people like us. You don't know them, they will put you in jail and you will never see daylight again in your life!'

'I don't care! You are making it up. Hindustanis also go there, I have heard about it...and what about those who carry the jhampans? If they can go, I can also go to the Mall,' he replied adamantly.

'Look, young man, the Hindustanis who go there and walk alongside the sahibs are well-dressed princes and princesses or the other royalties. How dare you compare yourself with them? Look at yourself and your clothes!' his uncle spat out. 'You are a poor hill boy. You haven't changed this kurta and pyjama for the last two months, nor have you taken a bath in weeks. You will be thrown out as soon as you are spotted there,' he added angrily.

Amrit Lal did not reply; he really wanted to see Mall Road and then a strategy formed in his mind. He would go in the night; there wouldn't be any memsahibs, but at least he would have a look around the Mall. A mischievous smile lightened his face.

'What are you thinking? You better leave as soon as possible, maybe tomorrow. I don't want to face the wrath of bhaiji if you land in trouble,' his uncle said, staring at him suspiciously.

'Chachaji, don't you worry. I will go in the night and see the Mall, no one will spot me there and then tomorrow I will return to the village.'

On hearing this, Mathu Ram violently shook the boy and slapped him hard.

'What have I done? Why are you so angry?' Amrit mumbled, not quite understanding the sudden change on his uncle's face.

'Angry? You fool! I am scared. If you do such a thing, you will never come back alive, people never return to relate their stories, their bodies are never seen, they disappear into thin air,' he screeched, trembling and shaken.

'What are you talking about?' The boy stared at him—had his uncle gone mad? He could not make any sense of what his uncle was saying.

'Evil spirits wander there, many people have confirmed this. Even the goras believe the same. Do you want to be eaten up by them?' Mathu Ram continued his outburst.

'Uncle, please sit down. I will not go there. I am going back to the village tomorrow as you say,' Amrit said, looking at his chacha's pale face. But this did not pacify his uncle.

'Tomorrow is too late. You are going today, pack your bags,' Mathu Ram said, exhausted by now.

In just an hour he was given a farewell by his aunt and cousin sisters, a packet of food (parathas and pickle) was handed over to him for his twenty-km-long trek. His uncle, who probably was still angry with him, did not talk to him after that.

Amrit, bewildered by the way he had been pushed out of the house unceremoniously, decided otherwise. After all, what was the need for his uncle to be so scared? This was *their* village, their Sheyamlah, they had a right to go anywhere and he was not a thief or beggar. As far as his being dirty and unwashed was concerned, he never had any lice in his hair as was the case with his friends and many elders at Ghanatti. Moreover, his clothes did not smell bad as he had worn a washed dress just a week before. He felt agitated and upset—his uncle who lived here, in proper Sheyamlah, and interacted with the firangis should not be so chicken-hearted to believe such nonsense.

For more than eight hours Amrit hid himself in the thick forest above Sanjauli. As night descended, he felt hungry and grouchy. He ate the parathas packed by his aunt and drank water from a stream nearby. He waited for another hour, and then started walking towards the Mall.

On the way he met two Hindustanis who stopped him and enquired about where he was going at this late hour, to which he replied that he was just strolling aimlessly, waiting for his uncle.

A fifteen-minute walk brought him to a wide open area which he thought must be the Ridge, as described by his uncle. Excited, he marched ahead. A great feeling of exhalation overtook him. He was there at last! There was no one around, he was the master of the place where the big sahibs and memsahibs walked! He wished he could see a mem and look at her white face and splendid clothes. He badly wanted to go back to his uncle's place and tell him that there was nothing to fear.

Amrit reached near Gaiety Theatre—it was a huge structure, with an intricate build and looked imposing. He was overawed. He was wondering where to go when he heard the sound of a horse trotting somewhere nearby. He remembered that his uncle had told him about the night patrol by soldiers. He must hide somewhere, he thought, and rushed towards the Mall from the Ridge. The sound of horses was closing in on him. He groped in the dark. Suddenly he saw an opening near the main gate of the massive building and entered inside. It was dark but he was not scared. All he wanted to do was—run away from the riding horsemen.

Amrit looked around, no one was visible. He saw a small spiral staircase leading to the basement. It was quite dark down there. He went down a few steps, unsure of where it led. Now he was nervous, but he decided to go downwards instead of returning to the Mall to be caught by the soldiers.

He continued to go down the staircase; it seemed unending. He stopped suddenly, remembering the spirit his uncle had warned him about. Fear gripped him. He saw two piercing eyes in front of him.

Amrit now wanted to turn back. Shaking with fear, he said, 'Oh Ram! Save me from the evil spirit.' But he could not get out. In his fear he tumbled down the stairs as if into an abyss. He felt as if he was caught by someone from the neck. Before he could react he was thrown against the wall. He hit the wall and slumped to the cold floor. He did not remember when he fell unconscious. When he opened his eyes it seemed like an eternity had passed. His head was aching and his entire body pained terribly.

Then he witnessed a bizarre scene. There was a round hall without any windows, in the middle of which was a big pit with a huge fire burning in it. There were two dishevelled men, both Hindustanis, pleading for mercy in front of two giant men—no...they were not men—who were dragging the sobbing men towards the pit.

One of the giants laughed and said, 'We have made a good catch. We will get enough ram-tel from their skulls.'

'Our masters will be so pleased. After all, this oil is the most effective tonic. It is a painkiller and heals wounds of the soldiers injured in war,' the other giant said.

Amrit was horrified when he saw that the giant hit one man on the head with an iron rod. He then tied the man's unconscious body on two rods hanging from the ceiling and hung the man upside down. His head was directly above the fire where a small pot was placed. At first Amrit wondered who had kept the pot there, then he saw a blue-skinned dwarf with protruding teeth and one horn on the head. The dwarf looked more dangerous than the giants!

He was left speechless and a voice inside him urged him to run from there, to return to Mall Road.

By the time he could react he heard someone whisper in his ears, 'Next it will be your turn, get ready.' Petrified, he turned back; the dwarf stood behind him with the most wicked smile on his face. Amrit was about to faint when the dwarf made a mark on his neck with a blue greasy liquid and said, 'I will come soon, do not leave.' The next moment he vanished, and Amrit saw him dancing near the fire where drops of black liquid were pouring into the pot from the head of the man hung upside down. One giant was looking at the hanging man amusedly while the other was getting ready to hit the second man with the rod.

God knows how Amrit got the strength but he got up and ran up the staircase. As he reached near the landing he looked back. His feet froze. He could not move an inch. His body was wet with cold sweat and he shivered. There was no fire there, no pit and no giants. He could not comprehend anything. One part of him wanted to go down again, but sanity prevailed and he ran upwards, and within minutes he found himself out on the Mall, and then he rushed towards his chacha's house.

ଔ

Anil shuddered with fear as the story came to an end on that cold night.

And this was not the only spooky tale he had heard about the theatre. The spirit of the business manager of the Amateur Dramatic Club (ADC) from the British era was a part of the folklore attached to this theatre. The Shimla correspondent of *The London Times* reported about the business manager of ADC, 'No one can believe the show would go on well without his ceremonial handshake and "wish you luck, sir" just before the curtain goes up the first night, his "*khincho*" (pull) heralding the lifting of the curtain by the brown attendants aloft and his "*chhor do* (let go), damn you!" which precedes the falling of the curtain. His motto is "it will be all right in the night" and he is most often right.'

Ram Rattan who worked as manager-cum-caretaker of the theatre for many years, maintained that the theatre was haunted and related his personal experience with the ghost of the long dead manager.

It was an unusually cold September evening that forewarned a long winter. Ram frowned at this thought as he shut the huge cast iron and carved wooden gates of the theatre. It took more than an hour after the show for the stage artists, helpers and their close aides to pack up and leave. After checking on the electrical appliances, he retired to his room and hit the bed.

A few hours later he was awakened by a sound; at first he didn't understand what interrupted his sleep. Dismissing it he closed his eyes again to go back to sleep; it probably is some old wood creaking, he thought. He could hear the wind howling outside. On the verge of losing consciousness to sleep, he suddenly woke up with a start.

This time he sat up—alert and wide awake. There was

no doubt about the tapping, now louder, now slower. The peculiar sound was rhythmic as if someone with a walking stick was tapping the wooden floor. He switched on the torch, looked at the watch on the side table, it was 3.20 a.m. There were only two possible explanations for the noise, either someone had been locked in or there was a thief prowling around the building.

Ram stealthily left the bed making the least possible sound with his bare feet on the old wooden floor, took the iron rod lying in his room and opened the door.

The tapping was still on. Relieved that the intruder had not yet been alerted he went down to the first floor cautiously. When he reached the bottom stair, he caught his breath—the intruder was coming towards him from the left side of the corridor. The caretaker held up the iron rod to strike if need arose. A few seconds later he stared in disbelief! The man was an old and well-dressed foreigner holding a hat. Before Ram could utter anything, the foreigner crossed him, brushing nearly against him and climbed up the stairs.

The tapping sound made by the walking stick brought Ram out of the trance and he followed the foreigner indignantly. 'Who are you? What, for God's sake, are you doing here?' he asked loudly. As he reached the second floor he was shocked to find that there was no one in the corridor! He stood there wondering where the man could have gone, and the tapping started again down below! Startled, he hurried downstairs again. It was just impossible, there was no other way from the second storey to the first storey, except through the stairs! When he stepped down he saw the foreigner coming upwards. He crossed Ram, climbing the stairs without a glance towards the terrorized fellow as if he did not exist. Then he heard the Englishman say in a heavy voice, 'Wish you luck, sir,' and then, '*Khincho...chhor do.*'

Ram understood that he wasn't seeing a man but a ghost from the past—thc ghost of the English manager who took care of the theatre; the one he had been told about by his predecessors. Throwing the useless iron rod there, he opened the huge iron gate and rushed out into the howling wind. An hour later a speechless Ram was found huddled in a corner by a policeman on duty!

The Ghost of the Lord and His Sister

'Prim Rose School?' she enquired suspiciously.

'Yes, aunty, the same,' Maggie said politely.

'But how could you get the job? Did they call you?' she asked; after all, her daughter, Sunita, was more intelligent and smart.

Maggie knew what aunty was thinking. 'I appeared in the interview,' she stated.

'Why didn't you tell Sunita about the vacancy, she could have applied too,' Aunt Sinha said accusingly.

'I did tell her, aunty, but that day she wanted to introduce her boyfriend to you,' she added cheekily.

'What is your plan? Will you be staying at the school? It is a boarding school, they must have teachers' quarters,' said Aunt Sinha, changing the subject tactfully.

'I don't know yet, I received the appointment letter only yesterday.'

Maggie bid farewell hastily. No doubt Aunt Sinha was irritating, but she'd made her think about her lodgings. She didn't want to shift to the school premises but she had been staying at her brother's place for too long, more than fifteen years since the death of their parents. It was time to move out. Her brother, a scientist at Potato Research Institute, stayed in a two-room government accommodation at Bemloi with his wife and two daughters. Maggie knew that there was no privacy for anyone in that small cocoon.

Now pondering about her future, she stopped at the vegetable shop to collect the items her bhabhi had asked for.

'It is good that you got the job, bibiji,' the shopkeeper said. She smiled. 'Now all you need is a good boy,' he added as an afterthought.

Maggie's smile froze on her lips. Marriage! It was all people were interested in. Why couldn't they understand that she didn't want to get married, she had even crossed the marriageable age. She was thirty-one.

'I have bought all the things you asked for,' Maggie said, placing the packets on the small kitchen table.

'What's wrong?' asked her bhabhi.

'What do you mean? Nothing is wrong,' Maggie snapped.

Reeta, her bhabhi, smiled. She knew every mood of her sister-in-law.

'Why don't you just ignore what people say,' she said softly placing her hand on Maggie's shoulder.

'Ignore! They are bent on butting their noses into my life, they need a tight slap,' she spat out.

'Maggie, you are no more a child, so act your age. How will you teach the young girls in school?' reprimanded her bhabhi with a twinkle in her eyes.

Despite her foul mood Maggie's face lit up with a small smile. Reeta was like a mother to her.

'I will go to the school tomorrow, there are so many things yet to be clarified like accommodation, rules for leave...'

'Accommodation! You mean you are going to get a house! And even if they do give you one, will you be able to stay there all alone!' exclaimed Reeta.

'Stop scaring me, bhabhi!' Maggie replied haughtily.

Everyone in her family knew that the slightest noise would make her jump in fright. Maggie was the source of much amusement and laughter due to this. She had never slept alone in a room. So, in a way, her bhabhi was right.

'I don't suppose there is going to be anything scary there. All that talk about ghosts is just a rumour. The room, if I get one, will be within the school premises and there are hostellers and other teachers living in the premises as well,' she added, more to comfort herself than her bhabhi.

'Don't even think of shifting, even if they ask you. As far as ghosts are concerned how many times have I told you that they don't exist,' Reeta said.

ꕤ

A month later Maggie joined the school. Along with her eldest niece she shifted to her new accommodation—a small room with an attached bathroom and a kitchenette. For Maggie it was an altogether new experience. This was the first time she was on her own. Until now, she had been living under the protective shadow of her brother's family. She had become very attached to them. But many a time she had felt the need to move out, build her own life and leave them to live theirs.

Then her niece returned to her parents. For nearly two weeks Maggie could not sleep alone in her new room. It was only the fear of losing her job which made her teach six lessons in the day despite having sleepless nights.

Her immediate neighbour was one Ms Mathai from Kerala. She had come to Shimla with her parents some thirty years ago. She was sixteen years elder to Maggie and had all the qualities of a good neighbour—considerate, helpful, jolly and carefree. She was not married—another thing they both had in common.

Slowly Maggie settled into her new lifestyle. It was customary to have pot luck dinner with her neighbour except on Sundays when Maggie left for her brother's place and Ms Mathai visited her cousins.

One Monday when Maggie came to school, she learnt from a teacher in the staffroom that Ms Mathai was not well and had taken sick leave. During the lunch hour Maggie dropped at her neighbour's to enquire about her health. She knocked at the door and without waiting for a reply, entered the room. It was dark inside with curtains drawn on both the windows. Ms Mathai was lying in her bed and staring at the ceiling. Her arms were placed under her head, and the upper part of her body was propped up slightly as if she was trying to 'see' something on the ceiling.

'Hello, ma'am! This is not fair, I go off to visit my brother and you fall sick!' Maggie said jokingly.

Ms Mathai shifted her gaze from the ceiling to look at her; for a second Maggie felt Ms Mathai had not recognized her, and then her blank stare was replaced by a feeble smile.

'What happened? Fever? You were fine when I left on Saturday...though after Friday night we haven't seen each other,' Maggie added as an afterthought. She affectionately held Ms Mathai's hand which was damp and cold.

'I don't know what the matter is. I feel very tired, sometimes cold, sometimes hot,' she replied weakly.

Maggie sat with her for another ten minutes, coaxing her to see a doctor and then she went to her room to make sandwiches for Ms. Mathai. She was late by two minutes when she reached her classroom, and thanked her stars that the principal hadn't come for the routine round. Later she attended the staff meeting and it was only after seven o'clock that she was free.

On the way while crossing Ms Mathai's room she heard voices coming from inside. One of the teachers must have called on her to enquire about her health, she thought and went to her own room. She had her usual cup of tea, tidied the room, bathed, which was her routine in the evening, and decided to cook something light and go to Ms Mathai's room with food.

At about 9.00 p.m., Maggie knocked at her neighbour's door, then pushed the door frame—it did not budge.

'Who is it?' asked Ms Mathai's weak voice.

'It's Maggie, ma'am, I have brought dinner for you,' a surprised Maggie answered.

A few seconds later Ms Mathai opened the door and stared into the blackness of the night behind Maggie.

'You are really unwell,' Maggie said in a worried tone as she entered the room.

Ms Mathai did not reply but bolted the door quickly. Maggie didn't know how to react. She had never seen Ms Mathai lock her door, sometimes even in the night when they retired. She had said there was nothing to fear since they were inside the campus guarded by a chowkidar.

Taking the plates out of the small cabinet in the kitchen she put together a serving of khichdi, a bowl of curd and some spicy chilly pickle.

'I think tomorrow you should see the doctor and then ask your cousin to stay with you till you recover,' Maggie said while handing her the plate.

'If it is what I think it is, no doctor or relative will be of any help,' Ms Mathai replied weakly.

A baffled Maggie kept her untouched plate on the side table. 'What is wrong, ma'am? You aren't behaving normally, bolting doors and this vague talk...I don't understand.'

'Just pray to God, let the evil go away, just pray, only prayers will help!' Ms Mathai babbled as if she had lost her mind.

Maggie felt fear grip her, what was Ms. Mathai talking about? What evil? The forgotten fear of the unknown and the dread of something inanimate came back with full force. An eerie silence reigned supreme in the room. Minutes ticked by, Ms Mathai kept staring at the ceiling while Maggie tried to grapple with the situation. Both of them had lost their appetite.

'You better leave, it's late,' said Ms Mathai at last.

'Yes. I will take the utensils tomorrow morning and in case you need anything or aren't feeling well, do call me,' said Maggie standing up, and carried the plates full of food back to the kitchen.

When Maggie closed the door behind her, she heard the bolting of the latch and Ms Mathai praying feverishly. Frightened, she began to walk towards her room. She had hardly taken a few steps when she felt a gust of wind on her neck and heard a whooshing hustle as if someone had passed her by quickly. Startled, she looked around but found no one. Her face went white and her mouth was parched. She stood terrorized as she struggled to decide whether she should go to her room or turn back and knock Ms Mathai's door for help. And then she heard the tinkling of a bunch of keys and along with it a swoosh like that of a dress. Relieved that it might be a colleague having an after-dinner walk or probably one coming to see Ms Mathai, Maggie called out for help. A few seconds passed; no one came. The sound returned again, this time quite distinctive: the juggling of several keys and a dress brushing against a wall or hedge; it became louder and came nearer.

Maggie stood petrified, she opened her mouth to scream but sobbed instead and turned back to her neighbour's room pounding blindly on the door.

It took some time before her shivering subsided in Ms Mathai's room, only to recur when her neighbour said in whispers, 'Did you see him too? He crossed you in a hurry and then later, his sister, who had a bunch of keys in her hand, passed too, with her gown flowing behind her, touching the nearby hedges.'

'Many times the children had told me about these two ghosts, I never believed them; it's been years, a century in fact, since the lord left!' she whispered.

'Who are they?' asked Maggie in a trembling voice.

'They are the ghosts of Lady Primrose and Lord Wilson. They roam about the area. The main building where we have the administrative block, was owned by Lord Wilson in the eighteenth century. It was his residence and he lived here with his sister. They loved the place so much that their spirits refused to leave the place.'

'Are they vengeful?'

'They aren't. They have never harmed anyone. It is another witch who resides here in the campus. She lives in a dungeon below the main building. Normally she stays there. But she comes out once in a while, maybe once a year on a moonless night. On Saturday I did not go to my cousin's place as they were out for a wedding. I decided to take a stroll outside after dinner since I was lonely. I think I saw her. And I am scared of her.'

'Oh!'

'Oh dear! She was in black and had red eyes on a chalk-white face. She crossed me and I heard her say, "I need blood, I am thirsty." I have heard that if you happen to come across her, she remembers you and comes to your bedroom through the ceiling and drinks your blood,' Ms Mathai said and then broke down.

Maggie, though scared, managed to say, 'Don't worry, she must have returned to her dungeon.'

'I hope so, they say she does not stay out longer than a night. But you never know,' murmured Ms Mathai.

The first thing Maggie did in the morning was to shift back to her brother's place and asked them to look for a husband! She didn't want the company of the chudail, the lord or the lady all her life!!

The Nakalchi Bhoot Who Died

Bhoot, rakshash and chudail are part of life here. They are as important in the social milieu as gods, devtas and devis. People eat, drink, play and dance with them. Here, there is no astonishment, surprise or shock that you interacted with a ghost or met a spirit. Like devis and devtas, the ghosts and witches have their area of jurisdiction over which they have full control. Trespassers are punished.

Welcome to a new world in Chopal in Shimla hills!

These spirits have different dispositions just like people. Some are harmless, some dispense justice, some lose their temper readily and some guard the water source, while some others are fond of forests. There are evil ones who attack people, too. Some demand respect; they want to be pleased before any important event. There are some who are mischievous, they love playing pranks. Then there are those who are forlorn and sad. Interestingly, some ghosts are rich, while some are poor.

Here, in this valley, you will meet Jeya ka bhoot who guards the water sources and the Maipul ka bhoot who scares everyone away.

And then there is Bras ka bhoot who is the chief justice for people living under his jurisdiction. In order to appease him a rot, one rupee is offered or a goat is sacrificed. When a theft happens in the village and there is a suspect, the villager confronts him and threatens him that if he did not tell the truth and return the stolen property he would call the Bras ka bhoot to dispense justice. The wrath of the bhoot is so greatly feared that the person accepts his guilt. And if he says that he did not steal anything, the victim usually believes him.

There is a bhoot who demands a payment whenever you enter its area. A separate area has been demarcated as his territory, where offering a one-rupee coin or a respectful namaskar if you do not have money, pleases him.

I came to this part of the Shimla hills looking for a ghost story, if only I could find one. But what I got is enough to fill reams of paper. I will share with you one of the most fascinating tales.

ᘓ

'This story is about a bhoot who loved to imitate humans. It is a real story but I don't think you will believe it,' the man said searchingly.

I nodded vigorously and said, 'Of course, I will.' These days I had become a believer of the paranormal. Moreover, I had to express this belief otherwise no one would tell me anything!

'This tale relates to my great-grandfather,' said the man who belonged to the Bahua parivar, an influential clan of the area.

'It happened long back, when my great-grandfather was young. He was gifted a piece of land by the Rana of our area for his services. This piece of land was away from the village and in the middle of a thick forest. The forest was full of bears, leopards and other wild animals. So my great-grandfather had to go there and spend the night on the plot to guard our crops. Otherwise, animals destroyed everything.'

I wanted to tell him that I was not interested in animals and crops, but kept shut as a mark of respect. He sensed my frustration and said, 'Have patience, you will get one of the strangest ghost stories, I assure you.'

He thus narrated his story:

So my great-grandfather Ganga Ram would go to watch the crop daily at night. He was not only the head of his family but also the only adult male in our joint family. He left home after dinner at about six o'clock for keeping watch. He carried one weapon with him, either a sword or a darat. Or sometimes a long stick for protection against wild animals. His other possessions were a *loiya* (woollen overcoat), a woollen shawl and a matchbox for lighting fire.

He had erected a temporary hut with four poles and a thatched roof. He sat for many hours on it, watching his fields. Every day he would build a small fire to keep himself warm and the wild animals at bay. Every few minutes he shouted loudly to make his presence felt and scare the animals.

The first time my great-grandfather saw it, he was intrigued. It appeared out of nowhere. It was not clearly visible but Ganga Ram knew it was there. He was not worried as he had put on the fire. Ganga Ram had already been told by many people that ghosts do not come near fire.

Ganga Ram pretended not to have seen the ghost and kept himself busy arranging logs in the fire and tidying his place where he would sit for hours to watch the crop. After some time when he looked up, the spirit was still there. He continued to sit in front of the fire and ignored the ghost. That night nothing happened, even though Ganga Ram felt uneasy in the company of the ghost. A few hours later the ghost rose and disintegrated into nothingness in front of his eyes.

The next day the ghost came again and sat there till 3 in the morning, then left silently as it had done the last day. This was repeated day after day. Ganga Ram did not notice any difference in the first few days, but later he realized that the form of the ghost was getting clearer by the day and soon it was fully visible like a real man.

Another amazing thing that happened was that the ghost had begun imitating his actions! When he moved his hand, the ghost did so too; whenever Ganga Ram stretched his legs, the ghost repeated the action. Ganga Ram noticed the actions of the ghost who would sit, get up, walk and make gestures of eating, drinking, smoking and even spitting just like Ganga Ram did. It was soon clear to him that this was a 'nakalchi' bhoot. Whatever Ganga Ram did, it would do the same. If he squatted down, the ghost squatted; if he adjusted his pattu, the ghost adjusted it too. If Ganga Ram looked towards the jungle, it too, looked that way; if he yawned, the spirit yawned, too.

It wasn't as if the ghost wore clothes, but it wasn't naked either. As his form became clearer, Ganga Ram noticed that the ghost wore the same clothes as him. He wondered how this had happened. Ganga Ram was amused. It was just an incredible timepass. However, after a few weeks, he began to feel irritated and soon his irritation gave way to exasperation and then anger. The ghost copied every small action of his—coughing, sneezing, blowing the nose, clearing the throat. The spirit imitated him even when he went to relieve himself.

And then the ultimate calamity struck. One day he spoke with anger, 'What are you, a fool?' Pat came the reply, 'What are you, a fool?'

The ghost had started talking too! Soon Ganga Ram dreaded going to protect the crop in the night.Though the ghost did not frighten him, it was always there imitating him, gnawing on his mind, eating his soul. He thought he would go crazy. He did not get any rest at night because of the imitations of the ghost. He did not sleep in the day either, for the very thought of facing him again in the night kept him awake. This restlessness began affecting his health. Then Ganga Ram started devising plans to get rid of the nakalchi bhoot. But no plan succeeded. The ghost was smarter than him. He had become bolder and was turning more human by the day. When Ganga Ram drank water from the lota, the ghost, too, extended his hand and drank water sitting a few metres away from the fire.

Life became hell for Ganga Ram and he would plan ways to get rid of this fellow day and night. He couldn't sleep or eat or do any work properly. He was the only male member in the family, the whole family was suffering because of him. He had tried all kinds of remedies—praying to devtas, changing his seating location—but all in vain. The nakalchi bhoot stuck to him like glue. And it had now started taking breaths as Ganga Ram did, it wouldn't be long before the bhoot entered his body and captured his soul. Something had to be done before everything was lost.

ଓ

Then one day he hit upon a plan. The next night he took ghee and *biroza* (resin) in two different vessels to the forest. He kept the two vessels in front of him as the ghost watched him cunningly. Ganga Ram smeared ghee on his limbs, arms and legs from the vessel placed near him; the nakalchi bhoot extended his hands and dipped them into the other vessel and smeared the liquid on his limbs, unaware that it contained biroza. Ganga Ram basked his hands on the fire and rubbed the warm palms on his body, and the ghost did so too. Lo and behold, it caught fire!

Ganga Ram jumped in joy. He had won the war against the nakalchi bhoot and thus become a legend.

ଓ

And that is how the nakalchi bhoot died giving birth to the popular saying, '*jahera bhoot aagiyo mua*' (the ghost killed himself in fire). People of the area ridicule and compare a person who acts foolishly with the nakalchi bhoot and warn that he would meet the same fate if he acted thus.

Nawab Comes Calling

It was a pleasant September night and Karam Chand was alone at night duty in Himachal Pradesh Institute of Public Administration. Since a couple of holidays had come together, most of the staff had gone on leave, combining their casual leave with the holidays and the coming Sunday. Currently, there was no training programme running in the institute, hence the place was very quiet.

Karam Chand belonged to Mandi, a buzzing town, and liked a lot of noise around him; so he felt uneasy being so alone. He was planning to go to sleep, when he glanced through the window and saw a man coming. At first, it didn't surprise him that someone had come in at 11 in the night. In fact, he was excited that he would have someone to talk to.

He got up to open the door and welcome the visitor. To his amazement, there was no one outside! He looked around, went to the front lawn but found no one and returned to his room a little dejected. Before going to sleep he glanced out of the window cursorily, and found that there *was* someone walking towards the building.

Where did this guy disappear when I had gone out on my search earlier? he thought. He opened the door and lo and behold, there was no one outside. Now he was irritated, he called out loud, 'Is there anybody out here?' There was such silence that you could hear a pin drop.

The story of the Nawab came to his mind, but he dismissed it. Now he was more alert and definitely a little scared. Nothing happened that night.

The next night he was on duty again, but this time he had the second chowkidar for company. They were talking to each other when, around the same time as the previous night, his colleague exclaimed, 'I can hear someone...who would be out so late in the night?'

Karam Chand felt an electrifying jolt; he had to investigate who was this man prowling on the campus. 'Come on,' he said, 'let's go.'

The other chowkidar was surprised by his charged demeanour. When they opened the door, there was no one.

'This is exactly what had happened yesterday! This

time I am going to catch hold of the intruder—man or ghost, whoever it is,' said Karam Chand firmly.

The second chowkidar looked anxiously at Karam Chand, 'Are you serious? Maybe the person has gone down to the village.'

'No, it is not possible,' Karam Chand said as he moved out. The second chowkidar shrugged and followed him to the lawns.

'Come on, yaar, there is no one here,' his colleague said at last. They had been walking all around for more than fifteen minutes.

Karam Chand was disturbed. How could someone disappear like that? There had to be some logic, he didn't believe the stranger had gone down to the village. No one walked so late, and the track to the village was away from the chowkidar's room; then why did the person come towards their room?

Then it happened. It was so sudden that Karam Chand was left speechless. A few metres ahead, to their left at the edge of the upper lawn, was a small canopy enveloped in a dull, monsoon fog. A man stood near it, wearing a huge fur cap and a long overcoat. He sported a long beard. Both the chowkidars stood transfixed as the man glided towards the canopy with his back facing them and sat down on the bench putting his legs on the railing and looked straight ahead, as if enjoying the night.

Karam Chand started trembling as he said, 'Oh God, it's

real.' It was the ghost of the Nawab. Then the figure stood up, walked a little towards the forest and then vanished into the blanket of darkness. Karam Chand looked at his colleague. To his consternation Karm Chand saw that he had fainted upon the stairs!

ଓ

It was 10.30 p.m. and Hem Raj was in the computer room in the second floor of the old building. It was an emergency. The director of the institute had left for Delhi early in the morning to attend an important meeting. Hem Raj was the personal assistant to the director. He had been told to type a couple of letters and take a printout of the expansion plan for the institute. Hem Raj lived on the campus in government accommodation.

He had hardly begun typing the letter when he heard someone walking in the corridor. Maybe the chowkidar has come, he thought, because when he had arrived there was no one in the chowkidar's room. He must have returned and come to double-check after seeing the lights on in the computer room. Unconsciously he waited for the door to open, but when for a few seconds nothing happened, he went back to typing the letter.

He had typed three lines when he heard the footsteps again. Someone was coming for sure. This time he called out loud, 'I am here in the room.' He did not get a reply, and there was no sound of footsteps anymore. And just as he started typing he heard the sound again, but this time the footsteps were retreating. It surprised him that the chowkidar did not even bother to come in despite his calling him.

He was irritated and mumbled something about the carelessness of the chowkidar when he heard the footsteps approaching the room again! This time he got up and opened the door. The corridor was empty! He stood confused. 'Where has he disappeared?'

There was no other room open, so he could not have entered any other room. And he wasn't imagining all this; he really had heard the footsteps clearly so many times.

He walked up the stairs to the chowkidar's room to enquire, but to his dismay no one was there. The room was locked. It must be him, Hem Raj thought irritatedly and went back into the building. As he approached the computer room he heard a sound coming from within as if someone was typing on a keyboard with force. Hem Raj felt uneasy; as he moved towards the door, the sound became more distinct, someone was actually typing.

Who could it be? Was it the chowkidar? But why would he do that? As he put his hand on the doorknob he felt a chill run down his spine. Scared to open the door, one part of his mind told him this was insanity and the other part advised him not to advance further. Then came the horror of horrors. He heard footsteps behind him. Terror-stricken, he forced himself to look back to find the source of the noise, and he saw a figure with a stick in his hand. He started trembling uncontrollably and was about to pass out when his vision cleared and his numb mind assessed that it was the chowkidar!

'What are you doing here, sahib?' the chowkidar asked. All he could mumble was, 'I...I...where have you been?'

'I was checking the hostels and when I came back I saw this room was lit and thought there was a burglar in here.'

Hem Raj sighed with relief. It must have been the burglar he had heard of. Of course, so stupid of him to think that there was some ghost around.

'What are you doing here, sahib?' the chowkidar repeated.

'I was...' Hem Raj was about to answer when he realized that the noise in the computer room had stopped. It was dead silent now. 'There is someone inside,' he whispered to the chowkidar. 'Probably the burglar!' he added anxiously.

'Oh!' the chowkidar replied, 'let us see.' The chowkidar opened the door and peeped inside, then he looked back at Hem Raj who had taken a few steps back from the door.

'There is no one inside, sahib.'

'What!' He couldn't believe this. Still petrified, he forced himself to look inside the room. The chowkidar was right. The room was empty. His glance fell on the paper he had left behind, it was not on the computer table he had been working on, but was now placed on a different table, and to his utter disbelief he saw the paper move, very little, but yes, there was movement. 'Run, run,' he said to the bewildered chowkidar as he ran out of the building. The letter was never written.

☙

I am in the library trying to find a document relating to the history of the institute. The librarian asks me exactly what I need. I find it odd to tell her that I am looking for some recorded incident about the ghosts in the institute, so I try to explain this to her in a roundabout way.

'You mean *chal,* an unexplained supernatural event?' she asks. I nod. 'Now there isn't any chal here, at least it is not visible and not as strong as it was earlier,' she says.

I am excited, at least she hasn't refuted outright the existence of ghosts in the institute. 'What do you mean?' I enquire.

'Well, after the havan things have become normal.'

'Havan? You mean you performed a havan here?'

'Oh no, it wasn't me! It was the institute.'

I am bewitched. The institute! How can an institute perform a havan? The lady explains, 'There were many strange happenings here, especially with the employees' families. Four to five deaths occurred, which remained unexplained. Many employees were falling sick and there were other strange things happening. People saw a wandering ghost of the Nawab and the spirits of a Nepali woman and a child walking around the campus.

'When the cooks heard the clattering of utensils in the kitchen, they thought everything might have crashed; but when they went into the kitchen they found everything in its place....

Then a famous pandit was summoned. He said that there were too many restless spirits in the area and that a yajna had to be performed to drive away the evil spirits. Each employee contributed ₹2,000 for the yajna. Seven nails of pure gold were made and taken to a shamshan ghat near Kairighat on the Shimla-Chandigarh Highway and dug there. This symbolized nailing the ghosts in the cremation ground.

'I hope the spirits rest there in peace now as we have had fewer incidents after that,' she concluded.

'Does this mean the spirits have been resettled from the institute to the shamshan ghat?' I ask. She nods.

'When was the havan performed?' I ask as an afterthought.

'In 2006,' she says matter-of-factly.

I am amazed—in this era, in this time!

The Muslim Ghost

This strange tale relates to a small hill village, Nankhari, near the old Hindustan Tibet Road at an approximate distance of 100 kilometres from Shimla.

With a panoramic view this spur of a mountain, which is home to many small villages, is a perfect location to spend some time in nature's lap both in summers and winters. To watch the early lemon sun as it glows on the snow-capped mountains, little terrace fields going down the valley and the deodar trees standing tall, is an experience to cherish.

Many British writers extolled the beauty of the valley located at a height of 8,500 feet, for its picturesque views and English weather. The two-room wooden guest house here is from the days of the Raj. At that time it was an ideal overnight resting place for the British officers on their way to Kinnaur. Its natural beauty and exquisite charm belies the existence of a ghost. Of this, the village folk tell an interesting tale.

ᴒ

One of my friends who belongs to this place, narrated this story to me. This ghost is not like the conventional ghosts. It didn't live here earlier, but came after Independence. This ghost is *owned* by a family, but despite my sincere efforts I could not talk to the family.

More than three decades have passed since the last fruitless effort was made to drive the ghost away to Lahore, its original abode. Moreover, it is not only the older generation who believe in its existence, but also the young and educated.

Thakur Sahib's family came from Lahore at the time of Partition and settled here in their ancestral village. He was a wealthy man possessing a lot of gold and jewellery which he had brought from Lahore.

Two popular explanations on how he came to possess this treasure are: he was a wealthy merchant in Lahore and before migrating he sold all his assets in return for gold. The other version is that his riches were a gift. Most of the villagers believe in the latter and state that a rich old Muslim woman had adopted him as her son. When the riots broke out, she gave him her family treasure to help him settle down in his ancestral village. And the ghost who guarded this treasure had to accompany Thakur Sahib. The local ghosts living in the area were not comfortable with the presence of an outsider ghost. But when they saw that the Muslim ghost kept to itself and stayed close only to the family, silently guarding the treasure, they let it be. So a pact of peaceful coexistence came into being among the ghosts.

Gradually Thakur Sahib's children got married and the ghost who was very attached to the older daughter left with her to her married home, located at a distance of about one kilometre from the house of her father.

Here the ghost decided to make his presence felt in the new locality and started disturbing people with new pranks every day. There were about twenty-five families in this locality when Thakur Sahib's daughter got married, but with the passage of time the number has decreased considerably. The main reason for this migration was the pranks played by the Muslim ghost. His tricks caused financial loss to the villagers, so many of them decided to move away from the village.

ଓ

My friend narrated several incidents about this ghost.

After dinner at their place, her maternal uncle had left for his own house located in a nearby village. He was advised to stay overnight since it was too late. He did not heed the advice and despite all persuasion, left for his home. Not more than fifteen minutes had passed when he came back screaming and pounded on the door like a mad man.

It was very difficult to pacify him as he stuttered and mumbled incoherently. For more than a week he was in utter shock and was bedridden. It was only after a month that he related the incident of that fateful night.

He had hardly walked a few minutes when he saw another person going in the same direction in front of him. He thought this must be some other villager and asked him to stop so he could accompany him. But this person did not stop and kept walking.

He increased his pace and when he reached alongside, he looked at the man. The man had a beard and a pointed nose and he had never seen him in the village! Before he could enquire, this unknown stranger started gaining height and, to his horror, kept growing taller and taller—so tall that he had to turn his neck at an odd angle to look at the person's face. He realized this was no human being, but a ghost or spirit. And he ran back screaming and crying for help.

'It was wearing a Pathani suit,' he added.

ೞ

The ghost appears even during the day and plays tricks with

the poor village folk. However, there is nothing sinister or life-threatening about its behaviour.

Funny are the pranks it plays. It drinks the milk of cows, the cows stop giving milk suddenly, and people have to sell the cow for peanuts, only to find later that the same cow had started giving plenty of milk.

'The veterinary doctor comes time and again, examines the cows and finds nothing wrong with them. He is unable to explain why the healthy cows stop giving milk all of a sudden,' my friend told me.

She told me that about three decades ago, the villagers decided to capture all the ghosts to end their 'reign' in the valley. They prayed to the local goddess to imprison the ghosts, including the Muslim ghost, and thus free the villagers from their daily nuisance. An auspicious day was fixed for the occasion. People from all the surrounding villages assembled in the large ground on the spur of Nankhari range.

My friend too had joined the crowd of villagers as a small child. It was an elaborate and expensive affair. More than twenty-five sheep were sacrificed during the ceremony to please the devi. Dancing and singing went on for hours. At the end of the festivities all those in whose houses the 'ghosts' resided were told to come in front of the devi and stand in a line. The devi, by now happy and in high spirits, talked to everyone individually and amidst the sound of drums and chanting, captured the ghosts. She took more than half a dozen ghosts with her and locked them inside her shrine.

However, the Muslim ghost was not captured because the daughter of Thakur Sahib did not stand in the queue when the 'ghost capturing' was taking place. The villagers knew that the Muslim ghost lived in her house, but due to her status in the village no one disclosed this to the devi.

Furthermore, the ghost had beseeched his owner not to disown it because it was a Muslim and could not live with the Hindu ghosts. It promised not to disturb anyone and stay in the house peacefully. But, after a few years, it went back on its promise.

The ghost still stays with the old woman and converses with her regularly. She, on the other hand, believes that its presence is a good omen and there is barkat in the house because of it.

Interestingly, the ghost wants to go back to its native place, Lahore. But there is a problem. It came with the treasure as the caretaker, now it cannot go back without the gold which has been liquidated over a period of sixty years. It has been given away in marriages of Thakur Sahib's children, and then further to the grandchildren. So the ghost is stuck here in India! Even though it wants to return to its hometown, the loyalty of the ghost towards Thakur Sahib's family is beyond question.

Once an old employee, an expert truck driver of Thakur Sahib, left the job for personal reasons. Thakur Sahib faced a major financial loss when one of his trucks driven by an inexperienced young man rolled down the mountainside. He tried to recall the services of his expert driver, but the man did not agree.

For no apparent reason this driver fell sick, and at one stage was confined to bed. He said that the Muslim ghost troubled him and was asking him to rejoin Thakur Sahib. For nearly three months the driver fought the persistent efforts of the ghost and begged it to leave him alone.

As a last resort, the family members of the driver took him to their local devi and asked for help since his health was deteriorating by the day. Even the local devi was helpless. She advised him to join Thakur Sahib's job. The deity claimed that the ghost would not let him live in peace. Since the ghost had a strong selfless devotion to his masters, even the devi could not intervene. A few days later when he had joined the services of Thakur Sahib, his health recovered.

ಐ

The most interesting bit is that my dear friend who narrated this tale in detail, was keeping a secret. Someone else mentioned this to me while I was researching. Later when I confronted her, she agreed.

This ghost, like other ghosts, enters a person's body every now and then. Once he'd entered the body of my friend. She was its victim when for two days the ghost stayed inside her and spoke about its desires, frustrations and helplessness. He remembered Lahore with nostalgia.

When the village head asked the ghost to stop troubling my young friend and leave her body, and to join a marriage party that was passing through the village, it said, 'Now I am too old, I can't run after marriage parties, they take you so far, a lot of my energy is wasted in coming back, this is not for me!' It also lamented that children had started making fun of it, teased it and disturbed its peace of mind because it did not belong to this place and had grown old.

No wonder my friend was so persistent in making me believe in the existence of Nankhari ka bhoot!

Viceregal Lodge

Viceregal Lodge in Shimla has two distinct histories—one can be found in history books while the other has been passed down from generation to generation. The original storytellers—the local hill women and men—told stories that had a thread of the supernatural woven intricately with the historical thread. Here, the tale is passed on through generations, which transports one to the times of the lords and the ladies...

☙

'What did he say?' asked the viceroy.

The aid-de-camp (ADC) shuffled, cleared his throat and bent his head downward, 'Nothing, my lord, you need not worry, it is just a triviality.'

Lord Lytton looked at his ADC and knew there was

more to what he was saying, but he was right: why should he worry about a local wanderer who blabbered non-stop in his native tongue, gesticulating with his outstretched hands towards the sky?

The sadhu saw the big sahib coming the next day again. He thought that it was important for this gora to know that two hundred years of British occupancy would come to an end. Here, at this very place, great leaders, some of whom were yet to be born, would gather in their fight for freedom. It would be here, again, that a decision of these freedom fighters would give rise to communal riots killing thousands.

'Listen to me,' he shouted as the party of the viceroy passed by.

'I know you cannot understand me, gora sahib, but when you lay the first stone in this place for your building, you will also lay the foundation of the revolt which will throw you out of Bharat. Mark my words.'

The party passed, no one said a word. The holy man had become a nuisance; his shrine had to be shifted from the Observatory Hill.

ଓ

'What troubles you, dear, did you not enjoy your evening walk?' Lady Lytton asked.

'Nothing, er...everything is fine,' he replied absentmindedly.

'Have you decided the place where the new viceroy lodge has to be built? So many more servants have died of typhoid here in Peterhoff. I think this place is not suitable anymore, and it is so small,' she complained.

'The Observatory Hill is a nice place, but I don't know why I am not yet sure.' He could not forget the sadhu and his blabbering; there was something he could not put his finger on. He decided that the next day he would set his mind at rest.

So the next day the viceroy, Lord Lytton, sent a fire balloon up from Observatory Hill. The balloon rose well and high to the relief of Lord Lytton. This sealed the place for the spectacular Viceregal Lodge. No one had dreamt that such a magnificent and lavish building could be made.

Lord Lytton at that time in 1878, called it 'a prospect so distant that it is only visible to the eye of faith.' Despite his best efforts he could not get the work started.

In June 1880, Lord Lytton was replaced by Lord Rippon. It was an abrupt appointment; the latter seemed satisfied with Peterhoff and did nothing to work on this project. It was Lord Dufferin (1884-1888) who added the Viceregal Lodge to the memorable architectures of the British era.

Lord Dufferin had first dreamt of building a castle on his Irish estate. But his own resources could not cover the expected cost, and his long-cherished dream came true at last in Shimla. It was one of the most flamboyant edifices of the British Empire and took two years to complete. The stones for the outer walls were brought on mules from quarries about eight kilometres away. For the building, tonnes of cut stones were transported on bullock carts from Kalka at the Shivalik foothills.

Utter confusion and chaos prevailed when Viceregal Lodge was being built. The retaining walls that were constructed a day before, were found in shambles in the morning. In the end, the viceroy agreed to the advice of a pandit who claimed that the place belonged to a sadhu whose spirit roamed around the area. Unless a small part of the land was left untouched in his memory, the spirit would not allow any building to be built. Thus a havan was performed, and even as the British watched it with scepticism and disbelief, the pandits chanted mantras on the Observatory Hill filling the atmosphere with the smell of incense and herbs. The land around the banyan tree adjoining the main building was kept aside for the spirit. Even now flowers grow there and nothing else has been built on the spot.

However, in the end, the forewarning of the sadhu came true! The decision to leave India was taken here in this building, which was once constructed as the symbol of the British empire motif. But it seems that this grand building was destined to remain haunted. So many people claim to have encountered British ghosts here. The night watchmen who guarded the building in the 1960s and

'70s slept in the main hall of the building and vouched that if they did not get up early in the morning, a loud, banging sound was heard on the main door and a deep voice rumbled, *'Uth jaao, subah ho gayi hai.'*

A retired employee told that he had heard someone walking on the first floor and sometimes on the stairs, but whenever they went to investigate they found no one. Another sound they heard distinctively was the noise made when electric switches are pushed.

'At that time, the switches were made of brass and made a distinct sound when you pushed them,' he said. So, on many nights this was a real irritant for the people on night duty. 'But what could we do? It was not in our power to tie the hands of the unknown spirits that reside there,' he said as an afterthought.

☙

'Since childhood, I wanted to work in this majestic building,' said the young man shyly, as he stood in honour of the elderly gardener. It was a privilege to meet this octogenarian who now came only once a year since his frail health did not allow many visits.

The elderly man wistfully looked at this young man; to him and to so many others, the British rule was an intriguing mystery.

'Oh! How I long to meet a lord,' the young man mumbled.

'We were not allowed to meet them, beta, we could only see them from a distance.'

'But how beautiful life in the big house must have been: the glittering lights, the parties, all those foreigners dressed in the best of attires...' He stopped abruptly; maybe he had said too much, giving flight to his dreams, which featured the lords and the ladies!

'Yes, the gora sahibs were so obsessed with this building and their lives in it that even now their spirits wander around here.'

'Spirits! You mean there are ghosts here,' said the young man, coming out of his reverie with a jolt.

His senior had lost interest in the rose garden, and had started to walk back to the main exit. He was a little irritated with himself for having revealed the 'secret' he had kept close to his heart for so long, to the boy. He stopped to look at the huge greyish structure that inspired awe and took your breath away. The lush green grass of various hues, immaculate flower beds, numerous ivy strands, yellow and white rose creepers clinging to the walls bespoke a relationship between the animate and the inanimate. The lawns were full of flowers: roses, daisies, buttercups, rhododendrons, fusia and geranium.

On one such April night when the flowers were in full bloom and the air was pungent with different kinds of fragrances, the old man had seen the ghost of the British lady three decades ago. He saw her when she was halfway through the spiral steps at the side of the main building—she had a lantern in her hand, her face looked so beautiful and radiant. She was wearing a white gown and walked elegantly. She crossed the whole terrace on the second floor of the main building, stopped for a few seconds at the end of the terrace and then turned, went back the same way, disappearing on the spiral wooden staircase, halfway through!

The old man was lost in memories. Some people said that it was the ghost of a Scottish lady who had died there, while others said that it was Lady Dufferin herself. He could not say which one she was, since he had no idea how the ladies looked!

If I Don't Eat, No One Eats

'No, you cannot refuse, Panditji, you have always blessed my children. She is the youngest, after that I am free,' Master Prakash Gautam said.

This was masterji's third visit in the last two days, but Pandit Padam Dev Sharma had politely refused, citing several reasons—there were many other good cooks in the village, people liked modern food whereas he was an old-fashioned *boti* (traditional cook). Moreover, in his advancing years he could not take the stress. But masterji was adamant.

A respected and influential landlord of a village near Darlaghat, at a distance of forty-five kilometres from Shimla, Pandit Padam Dev Sharma was a multifaceted personality. He was a renowned astrologer and a palmist, professional singer, musician by hobby and a seasoned gastronomer. For him, gaining knowledge was futile unless it could not be practised.

Till a few years ago he was the most sought-after chef in the area, but now he had started refusing offers. He wanted to devote the rest of his life to the study of astrology. But masterji was different—he was his childhood friend, and besides Master Prakash Gautam was his yajman too. But he was sixty-five years old, well past his prime and cooking food for a large gathering like a marriage party was no mean job.

'Make an exception for me, Panditji. You will have to take the charge. She is just like your daughter.'

'Please don't embarrass me. My health is deteriorating, otherwise I would have agreed readily. Allow me to guide you...'

'Your health is fine, you are an old guard. Don't be so adamant!' masterji said firmly.

'You are making this very difficult for me. People's tastes have changed. These days they like unhealthy, oily and spicy food. I won't be able to cater to such tastes.'

'I want what you cook, there is no match for it.'

'Okay, then traditional food it will be, and I want no interference, you know that,' Panditji said finally, knowing there was no way out.

'Don't worry about that, you are the boss,' masterji said, feeling elated. His worries regarding the meals were over. It was a very important aspect of the wedding.

Those were different times and marriage was not a one-day affair. So, it did not mean a single dinner or lunch, the baraat stayed for as many as three days. The food had to be not only tasty, but the guests demanded variety in the menu as well. Repeating a dish was not less than a sacrilege and people ridiculed the bride's clan for years for this botch. But then one could not spend unlimited money on food. Thus the head cook was required to be not only imaginative, but also parsimonious.

Pandit Padam Dev was not just a great boti, he was a magician when it came to cooking. And the best part was that he was frugal too. Only he could transform ordinary vegetables and pulses into a delicacy with the least possible condiments.

Once he had cooked in the marriage of a poor villager's daughter. The baraat overstayed due to bad weather and Panditji served them with masoor dal, *khatta mahni* (accompaniment of raw mangoes) and hot fluffy rice. Instead of complaining, the baraatis showered praises on him for the delicious dal. Not only that, Panditji cooked pumpkin in six different styles for the other round of meals and the baraatis relished the food thinking that those were all different vegetables. At the time of their departure they requested the girl's father to honour the head boti so they could convey their pleasure. The embarrassed Panditji was given two rupees as shagun by the groom's father.

For Panditji, cooking food was a sacred ritual and he had his own set of rules and regulations which he stuck to. He was a strict taskmaster and a stickler for discipline, punctuality and hygiene. No one could enter his spic-and-span kitchen that was mostly set up in the open.

Panditji's assistants started the preliminary preparation five days before the first meal was to be served. The first three days were devoted to buying and storing the essential commodities and setting up the kitchen. The next day Panditji checked supplies personally and performed a small puja at the kitchen site, and the assistants started cutting and peeling off the vegetables. He would plan so meticulously that every dish would get ready just at the time of the arrival of the baraat.

The menu of the main *dham*, the traditional festive food, was always the same. The sweet dish was served first. It could be yellow sweet rice with dry fruits cooked in pure ghee or bedana-boondi in sugar syrup with lots of dates and coconut. The main menu consisted of rice, puri, two dals including mash ki dal, a vegetable and a khatta dish, which could be the popular kadi with pakoras or spices and bundi mixed with curd, or a thick syrup made of lemon, tamarind and bundi. For breakfast, it was either puri chhole or puri aloo.

ର

The baraat was to arrive by noon, but as is the case in all marriages it was not expected to reach before 2 p.m. A group of children with a ringleader had been positioned at the village quila, atop a small mountain, to report the arrival of the baraat, especially to those managing the kitchen.

'Is everything prepared, Panditji?' a hassled and tired masterji on his way to the aangan asked.

'Take it easy, you don't worry about the food. Everything is ready. I will put the dishes to heat in time so that they remain hot. Rice will be ready by the time your guests arrive,' Panditji said, but masterji was no more in sight—someone had taken him away. After all, he was the father of the bride, a busy man.

The open kitchen set up at the backside of the house was orderly, organized and clean. Four huge vessels nearly full to the brim were on fire. A group of five helpers, long-time companions of Panditji sat around, seeping the warmth of the glowing logs. Relieved but anxious, they would be at rest only after the food was served and appreciated.

While they were chatting squatted around the fire, a young man appeared before them suddenly.

'Yes, boy? What are you doing here? Go to the house, the baraat will be reaching soon,' said one of the attendants casually.

The man did not move, he gaped at all of them one by one and then at the food placed on the fire. One could not guess his age from his face. An ageless and strange face, panditji thought; he was bewildered. Something was wrong. Who was this boy and what was he doing there?

'Who are you? You are not from this village, are you?' panditji asked him.

The man's gaze was fixed on the vessels; he betrayed no sign of having heard Panditji.

'This is the kitchen and no one is allowed to step here. You must leave right away,' Panditji added brusquely.

The boy glared at Panditji who cringed involuntarily as if trying to save himself from a blow. A shiver ran through his body.

'I am hungry, give me food,' the boy said.

'Hungry! Just run away from here. There is a marriage going on and this food is for the baraatis,' one of the assistant said rudely.

'I said I am hungry, I have not eaten for three days. Give me food. All your vessels are full of food,' the boy said in a strange tone.

'Why don't you sit down, we will give you a cup of tea. You can have as much food as you want after the baraatis have eaten,' Panditji said, trying to pacify the boy.

The man stared intently at Panditji again, and then sat down. One assistant poured the hot sugary tea in a steel glass and handed it to the stranger.

'Which caste do you belong to?' asked the helper

suspiciously. The man did not reply but drank the tea hungrily.

'The baraat has come...the dulha has arrived,' the news spread like fire in the small village on that December afternoon.

Then the cooks got busy giving final touches to the dishes. Suddenly the man got up and demanded agitatedly, 'Give me food, I am hungry.' Startled, everyone looked at him again.

'Are you deaf? Hasn't Panditji told you that the baraatis will have the food first, no one eats before the guests,' said one of the attendants.

'No, I want it right now.' The boy was obstinate.

'Have you gone mad? Don't you understand what we are saying! Run away before I throw you out,' another cook said angrily.

The boy scowled and stared at them all, one by one. 'If I don't eat, no one will eat,' he said and walked off.

'I think he is drunk, you never know what kind of people you may come across these days,' said one of the cooks.

The loud drumming of dhols punctuated with shrieks of giggling girls floated from the house. The baraat had arrived.

Soon the food was to be served. But then a catastrophe happened—all the dishes got cold. The fire was burning, the vessels were hot but every dish was cold from the inside and the rice was uncooked. What did this mean?

In a matter of minutes chaos reigned in the kitchen. Confused, the cooks looked at each other helplessly and then at Panditji. How could an experienced man like Panditji not be able to prepare food in time? Elders from the girl's side, including the mamas demanded answers. They looked at Panditji with accusing eyes. Half an hour passed, the baraatis got restless and there was tension in the air. But the dishes continued to remain cold despite the burning fire underneath the vessels.

Then Panditji remembered the boy and his cold stare, and realization hit him. 'Call that boy who wanted food,' he shouted at his assistants who fanned out in all directions to look for the stranger who had said: 'If I don't eat, no one will eat.'

'That man has made the fire lose its warmth, he tamed the fire cold,' said Panditji to himself.

Fortunately, the man was found near the village bowli and brought to the kitchen. He was made to sit down and was served water. A few minutes later food started bubbling in the vessels and when it was placed on his plate it was piping hot and well cooked. The surprised attendants served him well. He ate to his heart's content.

The agitated baraatis were pacified and served food an hour late. However, the taste and quality of the food made them forget the delay, and the marriage was solemnized peacefully.

The stranger left the place as quietly as he had come; no one knew who he was or where he went. Panditji could not forget that face. It was the last time that he cooked food—for a wedding.

The Hand

It is so difficult for me to tell you what had happened; believe me, I am neither a coward nor a superstitious person.

I was born and brought up in a liberal and modern family. My father is a doctor and mother a teacher. I did my schooling from one of the most prestigious and oldest schools of Shimla. During my childhood, I had heard numerous tales, stories and folklore about the haunted and the supernatural. Somehow, it was all part of the mysteries of growing up: these tales brought cheer to our lives (studying in an all-boys school, we didn't have enough topics to discuss), and our group of friends would narrate to each other the hearsay and the folklore attached with the school—the faceless ghost, the headless ghost, the ghost on the horse, the ghost in the laboratory, and so on.

To tell you the truth, though we were scared and believed these stories to be true, somewhere at the back of our minds we were aware that none of our friends had actually seen a real ghost. Perhaps some other boy had, or a senior, or for that matter someone from years or decades ago, whose encounters were told and retold and became a part of the history of the school.

To me all these were fables, sometimes real and scary, sometimes interesting and at other times, just matters to be laughed at. My belief in the existence of ghosts switched like a pendulum, depending on the time of the day the story was told, on the narrator who had 'actually' seen the spirit, and similar other factors. In a way you can say that I grew up being acquainted with and appreciating these haunted tales, and thus being aware of their existence.

One other essential thing I would like to confess is—I enjoy my drink, but I am definitely not an alcoholic. I am married and stay with my parents. A drink or two with my dad or my visiting friends before meals is not unusual.

Now I come to the real part of this story—the incident which changed my outlook and shook me to such an extent that I became a believer, of both God and the supernatural.

☙

It was a beautiful April day, crisp and cool. Flowers were blooming, spreading their fragrance around. I had woken up to bright sunlight, chirping birds and singing butterflies after a restful sleep. The landscape was full of colours and I could not stop tapping my feet to the song of my heart. It was one of those days when you felt immense love for God's creation. The whole day I was buoyant and joyful, overwhelmed with the magic of being alive. I had planned to take my wife Shilpa out for dinner, but I got to know that a few of my parents' friends were coming for dinner and so Shilpa would be tied to the kitchen. On an impulse I called my friend Sumit and invited him for dinner at Hotel Holiday Home (HHH).

Sumit and I studied together in school. He was working in Delhi and had returned to Shimla after nearly two years, so we had a lot of catching up to do. Sumit was the only bachelor left in our group, though he had a steady girlfriend of more than seven years. By the time we reached HHH, it was already 9.30 p.m. I knew my family would be busy dining with the guests till 11.30 in the night, so I wasn't particularly worried about reaching home on time.

After exchanging pleasantries, we sat down and watched the lights of Shimla town twinkle along with the yellow-white light of Christ Church flaming in the corner, from the window of the restaurant. We were about to order our drinks when the quiet ambience was shattered.

A group of twenty to twenty-five rowdy tourists entered the restaurant. The scraping of chairs, the giggling and babbling, the summoning of waiters who anxiously gathered around them, brought so much discord and disquiet into the restaurant that I suggested we go to my place. Sumit would also be able to meet Shilpa and my parents, and we all could have dinner together. The waiter who had served us water hardly looked at us when we were leaving; he was busy taking care of the tourists.

Just as we settled into the car, I impulsively suggested to buy a bottle of whisky so we could enjoy a drink or two on the narrow lonely road which led to our old school. It was a beautiful night to spend outdoors. We reached the upper gate of the school at about 10.30 p.m.

I had just parked the car and was opening the cork of the bottle when Sumit's mobile phone rang. It was his girlfriend calling; he excused himself, got out of the car and moved a few metres behind the vehicle. In the closed vehicle, I was sitting in the driver's seat and could vaguely hear his side of the conversation.

I had not yet opened the bottle and was just toying with the cork, waiting for my friend to finish his conversation, when I felt that there was someone in the back seat. First, I wanted to turn my head and look behind, but then I thought there couldn't be anyone there since my friend was outside.

Then I found myself talking to the person sitting in the back seat. It was strange, but I was doing it. I knew there was no one in the car, but at the same time I also knew there was someone with whom I was conversing.

It sounds crazy now, but at that time it seemed perfectly normal. The conversation continued for some time. All this while, I was toying with the cork and the bottle was tucked between my legs.

I spoke to the person sitting at the back, but I don't remember what we talked about. And you know, I was conversing with him in a strange way: while I was speaking loudly, that man was not actually 'speaking', but I heard him clearly in my head. It seemed like telepathy—he was 'talking' to me. Suddenly I said out loud, 'Who am I talking to? There is no one in the car!' And then I felt a hand clutch my arm below the shoulder from inside the jacket!

I remember the touch clearly. It was real. It had the pressure of a normal human hand and its feel was also similar. I could feel each finger, the thumb and the palm exert pressure on my arm. A gentle, friendly pressure. But I also knew that it was something unnatural since there was no one else in the car. I swear I was numb with shock. All this while 'he' kept on 'talking' to me in a soft, musical voice.

The spell was broken when my friend suddenly opened the car door. I immediately jumped out of the car; the bottle fell down, but I did not care. I rushed out of the car and flung open the back door, angrily demanding, 'Who is in there...come out!'

'Who are you talking to? There is no one in the car!' my friend said, bewildered.

I was nervous, perplexed and agitated. I had been talking to that 'someone' a while ago!

I asked my friend how long had he been on the phone. He said, 'Fifteen to twenty minutes.' An eerie feeling arose in my heart. I had talked to that 'person' in the car for as long as my friend had been on the phone but I couldn't remember what we discussed. I shuddered, no words came out of my mouth. I clutched the door of the car to support myself. My friend saw that I was unusually disturbed and understood that something had transpired in his absence. He took charge and made me sit in the car. He drove me home. I spoke to no one and went straight to the puja room.

I did not sleep that night and at the break of dawn, I rushed to our native village to pay obeisance to our kul devta. From that day onwards I was transformed into a different man, believing in the unknown and the power of God to give you peace and solace during turmoil.

ଓ

Later I got curious and tried to find other people who had had similar experiences. To my surprise I met many such people. One such strange tale was narrated by a friend to me:

Something creepy happened to me for the first time in my life. It was 13 December. I was invited to dinner at a friend's place near the Radisson hotel. My husband was out of town, so I told my friends, who were invited as well, that I would come on one condition—if they drop me back till New Shimla, where I reside. After completing the day's task, I parked my car on the road near a famous Shimla school.

After dinner we reached close to the school in my friends' Bolero, discussing the Special Olympics which were to take place two days later in the school grounds. We were one of the organizers of that mega event.

My friend Radhika suddenly announced that she was having a headache. I had some medicines in my car. The group had to take a round of the school to ascertain if everything was all right—three hundred participants and organizers were putting up in the campus. I told Radhika that I would give her the medicine and then they could all go down to the school while I would return home.

The narrow road, from the chowk to the parking area in front of the school gate, was lined by a wild forest on both sides. My car was parked about a hundred metres away at the other end of the road. When I got down and started walking towards my car, I felt scared. The area looked deserted and the silent trees with their shadows looming large gave an eerie feel to the place.

However, ignoring my fears, I reached the car and opened the door opposite to the driver's side where lay my daypack. While I was rummaging through the bag trying to locate the medicine, I felt uneasy, as if there was someone in the car. Now I was definitely nervous and jittery. Moreover, there was an unexplainable urge to hurry up, find the medicine, give it to Radhika and just get away from the place.

I remember telling myself that I was being stupid. Then I heard someone say 'Hello'. The first thought was: what in hell was Radhika doing...saying hello to me! Naturally, I speculated that she had followed me to the car.

I looked behind my shoulder to retort, only to find no one there! Stupefied, I hurriedly closed the door, walked back to the Bolero on shaking legs to tell Radhika that I did not have the medicine, and asked my friends not to move from the place till I had driven away.

I walked back panic-stricken, telling myself this was all nonsense! I opened the driver's door and sat down inside, and when I started the car I again felt that there was someone in the car sitting next to me! I don't know whether I was numb with shock, in a trance or too scared, but I pressed the accelerator, turned the car and drove like a maniac knowing that whatever 'it' was, it had power only in that area. I have never driven so fast in my life and it was a miracle that I did not skid, bump or have an accident!

Now the more I think about it the surer I am that the 'hello' I heard was not imaginary. I was not hallucinating. It was clear. Though, at first, I had suspected it was Radhika, I later realized it could not have been Radhika at all. It was a soft, male voice with a clear English accent. It was a sing-song voice moving with the wind that came from far away, but was near at the same time. In fact, it practically touched my ear. And when I looked back at my shoulder, the image that flitted across was of an Englishman—very thin, wearing a long coat and a hat, holding a baton!

Yes, he was there, greeting me with a longish 'hello'.

The Rising of the Dead

I am perplexed. How should I tell this to my husband or my father-in-law? I have tried to ignore the incidents for more than a month, but now it's eating me up. I will go crazy thinking about it. There is no other option but to tell them about *it*...well, er, about *him*. The day I saw him for the first time I thought he was a figment of my imagination, but not anymore. This can't go on, I am too disturbed, and to tell the truth—scared out of my wits.

ꕥ

I am Anupama, twenty-six years old and belong to Chandigarh. I met Happy in Punjab University—he was doing law, and ours was a whirlwind romance. In three months we were married and I accompanied him to Shilaru, a hill village in Shimla district, my new home.

For one year, our married life was blissful. We would regularly go to Chandigarh on a whim for an outing, for shopping, dinners and even for buying groceries. On the spur of the moment we would decide to go to Chandigarh to eat at Subway, or for rasmalai at Gopal's, or watch a movie in the new mall.

Gradually, the freshness of our marriage fizzled out, and with that, our trips reduced. And now it has been more than six months since I had gone to Chandigarh. However, I don't crib about it. I am happy and satisfied with his affection. Sometimes I feel that this change in him is abrupt and unnatural. At times he is his earlier self—carefree, passionate and joyous—then suddenly he seems so withdrawn and aloof. I don't know...there is indeed something unexplainable.

My in-laws are agriculturists and I am aware that my husband will have to be here to take care of the family business. He had thought about practising law just on a whim, but serious practice was not his cup of tea.

I have two sisters-in-law, who are happily married in the vicinity. My mother-in-law is a little different. She stays more at her parents' house in Kumarsain than with us. She says that she does not feel well here, and falls sick when she is in this house. She is a quiet woman and an introvert. My father-in-law is a very active man. He is like a second father to me. He is the backbone of the family, looking after both the apple and cherry orchards, and the polly houses—the home of off-season vegetables.

So this is my family. We have no problems and everything is fine, but in the last six months, somehow an undercurrent of malevolence has crept in. I cannot put a finger on it, maybe I am just paranoid.

Things changed dramatically a month ago. I practise yoga from about 4.45 a.m. to 6.00 a.m. before the family wakes up. I have been doing this for the last ten years. It is a habit that I can't let go of, come snow or hail. After completing my morning yoga, I get busy in the kitchen and other household chores.

It was a Saturday, and I remember being watched even while doing yoga. Thus, involuntarily, I had looked back twice to the bed where my husband was sleeping, thinking he had woken up and was looking at me, but he was deep in slumber, with a quilt over his head.

When I went to the kitchen at about 6 a.m. to make tea for all of us, I felt someone standing at the kitchen entrance again. I turned back, only to find no one there. But this time the feeling was very strong. Someone was definitely gazing at my back. Initially this didn't frighten me, it irritated me. Was it my father-in-law? But why would he do such a thing? For the next few minutes I was uneasy. After I had made tea, I looked straight at the window and, yes, there was a blurred figure. I could not make out the features. Since it was snowing outside, everything was already white, and this figure was white and grey! I immediately turned to look at the kitchen door hoping that Happy or papaji had woken up but in vain. Then I shifted my gaze back to the window, and this time I couldn't find anyone out there. That was it. Just snow falling heavily.

I did not think much about this—either someone from the village was passing by and had stopped outside the window, or it was snowing heavily and, unable to see clearly, I had just imagined it all.

About two weeks later we had gone to a distant relative's house. It wasn't very late, around six in the evening; darkness was descending. Happy left for the market to buy some vegetables, and I started for home.

I will tell you something about my house: it is a two-storey building, one kilometre down from the national highway at Shilaru. A narrow link road connects it to the house. There are a few other houses in the vicinity which are visible but every one of them must be about 300 metres apart. The house is perched on a small hilltop which looks down into the Shilaru valley and in front to the vast bijli dhar, a virgin forest mountain. The rising and setting sun embraces the house from morning to evening. It is a warm home.

While coming down from the national highway to the link road, there comes a dilapidated structure. It has crumbling walls—a proof that it was a small house long ago or maybe a cowshed or bhandar.

This time when I crossed the cowshed, I felt someone watching me. I was definitely frightened. The looming darkness and being alone out in the open fed my imagination further. I panicked. I glanced back over my shoulder and finding no one, increased my pace. But the watching eyes would not leave me. I started running now. I had never run like that ever. I met my father-in-law just outside the house. He was surprised, but I could not tell him what had happened. It did not make sense. For the next few days I was perturbed and did not venture out of the house. Later I got immersed in the daily chores and forgot this strange experience.

And now it had happened the third time. It was a Saturday night again. Happy and my father-in-law were working on the accounts. They did this once every three or four months; it took them a couple of hours to finish their work. By the time we had dinner it was 12 o'clock and I had just finished tidying up the kitchen when I felt 'those' eyes watching me again.

This time there was no doubt about it. It was definitely not a figment of my imagination as I had told myself earlier—I was frightened to death. I wanted to scream for help, holler for Happy to come at once. But I felt powerless. I dared not to look anywhere; I was transfixed, and, of course, I did not want to be alone in the kitchen. My legs were shaking; I heard myself whimper and unconsciously started muttering my devi's name. I had never chanted our kul devi's name. Soon I realized that my chanting had given me the strength to coordinate my movements again. I looked behind me, knowing that there was no one. I was right.

At that instant I turned towards the kitchen window intuiting he was there, and yes, he was! It was a full-moon night and he was clearly visible this time. A man's form clad in a grey coat but with blurred features. I was petrified and I could hear my heart beating irregularly against my ribcage. A silent scream of horror escaped my mouth. On wobbly legs, eyes locked with the man's figure, I slowly stepped backward and ran to our room from the kitchen door, exhausted and terrified. This was last night.

☙

There was no other option. I had to tell him. However, Happy did not take it seriously until he told this to his father. Well, thank God, papaji did not laugh at me!

It was not something to laugh at. Mr Chauhan was, in fact, intrigued. The child had no idea what was going on in their family, he thought. He must call the devta home to get rid of the evil spirit.

☙

I am exasperated, and for the first time I feel like an outsider. No one tells me anything directly. In fact, Happy is uncommunicative. A few days after I told him about the apparition, Happy said that the devta would be called and the family would pay obeisance to him—there was going to be a large gathering of people, songs and dance, a lamb would be sacrificed as well. As far as I was concerned, I thought it would be great fun. A change from the routine, I, too, now believed in Happy's devta and wanted to do my best for the deity. And then a day before the ceremony, the plans changed. Happy came to the kitchen; he looked devastated.

'What is wrong?' I asked, alarmed.

'Everything,' he blurted out. His statement shook me. I told him to sit down, calm himself and tell me everything.

'What is there to tell? Devta will not be coming,' he said bluntly and left the kitchen.

I knew that since I had spoken about the apparition, there was a lot of hush-hush going about the house among relatives, neighbours and the pandit, gur (spokesperson) of the devta. People came and went, and to my frustration talked in whispers. Then it was announced that the devta would be visiting the house, and now that too was cancelled. I was at my wits' end and decided to confront my father-in-law.

ଓଃ

'Well, child, since you say you don't understand what is happening, I will tell you everything. This is how things stood before you told Happy about what was happening to you ...' he trailed off.

'You mean what I saw,' I stated directly.

'Yes, er, what you saw. It's the spirit of...'

'Spirit,' I said horrified, growing pale.

'Why don't you sit down...I will explain everything to you. Happy doesn't understand,' he said, gently coaxing me to sit on the stool and to be courageous to accept what he was saying and understand its complexity.

'You were not the only one who was going through this unusual time. I also experienced the presence of the spirit,' he said lamely. I sat bolt upright now.

'Yes, a couple of days before you revealed your experience, small but significant things were happening around us. I don't know if you noticed. Your mother-in-law gets unwell whenever she comes here. Happy has lost all interest in business. He sits listlessly at home. The crop in our orchards is failing, and the hailstorm hits only our orchard. We are losing money on each one of our investments. The cows don't give milk regularly. On a number of occasions I have felt someone following me. I discussed this state of affairs with the village elders and they told me that the devta should be called. But then something happened yesterday—my cousin had gone to the gur's house when the devta entered his body and told him that it was 'paap'. And when 'paap' wants to remind you of your follies, this happens,' he whispered.

'What?' I said, getting up from the stool, my heart hammering hard.

'Sit down, don't be...'

I started crying, I could not help myself.

'It is nothing, child, it is not our fault.'

He explained what this meant, 'Paap means that when the spirit of an ancestor haunts you, it becomes *pitr-dosh*. An ancestor whose soul is not in peace, or who died dissatisfied, or whose rites were not performed properly comes back in the family after two or three generations and demands respect.'

'How do you know?'

'The devta told us. Besides the elders know that the *pitr* of my great grand-uncle has come back. You remember that house on the way...'

'The one with crumbled walls,' I mumbled.

'Yes, it belonged to my great-grand-uncle. It is his spirit's home now, and all these supernatural encounters that we have experienced are its way of making us acknowledge its presence,' he explained.

'What do we do?' I asked terrified.

'First, I will go to Haridwar and perform his last rites, and then a small stone idol will be made and kept in the house. We will have to give respect to this idol and pay obeisance to him.'

'How do we do that?' I asked.

'Well, on every festive or important occasion he has to

be greeted first and the food is to be served to him before others. Any guest who comes to our place has to greet him first and one has to ask his permission for important things.'

'He would be just like the eldest in the house,' I said, feeling less terrified.

He smiled and said, 'You are right. But my son does not understand this. With his modern education he thinks these things are just figments of human imagination. But we know that these supernatural beings do exist. You should try to make him understand,' he added, patting my hand.

Was this natural? I asked myself and instantly got a reply: 'Of course! It is a part of life here and has been going on for hundreds of years.' I am relieved. I can handle this. Giving respect to the elders—no problem!

The Haunted Mansion

'How long have you lived, Dadaji?'

'Lived? I am still living!' he said, laughing.

'But for how long?' the small girl studying in third standard asked again.

He was eighty. How long would he live was a more important question, he thought.

'Tell me, Dadaji!' Deepa screeched this time.

'For many years, child,' he replied.

'Forty years?' she asked tentatively.

Malkiat Singh laughed pulling his favourite grandchild into his arms.

'Tell me, Dadaji, forty years?' the small face looked up at him seriously.

'Why are you asking this?'

'I want to know something about Shimla. If you have lived here for many, many years you will know everything. Teacher *ne kaha boodhe logon se poocho,*' she replied earnestly.

Malkiat grunted in disgust, there was no respect left for the aged. If teachers talk like this, what would the children learn from them? What was the use of sending children to expensive schools?

'Did your teacher say *"boodhe log"*?' he asked, visibly upset at the teacher's brazenness.

'Dadaji, look, this is what my teacher has written in our notebook.' She thrust her notebook into his lap.

The notebook had the following comment: Ask old people about the past of Shimla and write an unusual story based on their experience about the old Shimla. The note was for the parents rather than the child. What stupidity! Malkiat thought, and decided to go to the school to show the note to the headmaster.

'Will you tell me the story?' the child asked in a pleading voice.

'I will, but let me think.' There are so many unusual tales about this place. Should he tell her the mysterious stories of Shimla, he wondered.

ଓ

The fate of Shumlah, a tiny hill village, took a dramatic turn in the first half of the nineteenth century when a white man 'discovered' the hill station to have English weather and decided to call it home. The Gerard brothers were the first to arrive here. These two Scot officers were engaged to survey the Satluj Valley and they mentioned a 'middling size village (Shumlah) where a *faquir* gives water to travellers' in their diary on 30 August 1817. But some chronicles attribute the discovery of Shimla to Sir William Lloyd in 1821 or to Lieutenant Ross in 1819, while some to Captain Charles P. Kennedy in 1822.

It was Charles P. Kennedy who made a permanent house here. But this, too, is debatable. Some researchers say that the first house of Shimla was the house near Christ Church, presently called Siddhowal Lodge. It was constructed in 1826 and was called Bally-Hack and later, Christ Church Lodge. Whosoever may be the builder of the first house, the village went on to become the summer capital of the British.

During the time of the British, summers in Shimla were synonymous with festivities. Polo, picnics, moonlight parties, balls, theatre, fetes and hunting trips, all filled the time. As winters approached, the imperial fancy ended with sadness and the visitors disappeared for a few months deserting the hills to return in summers. After months of romance, flirtations, partying and cacophony, Shimla returned to its simplicity and slumped into wintry slumber.

As the paraphernalia of government descended to Indian plains, following the annual ritual, so many others got ready to leave the cool hills—prostitutes, quacks, magicians, jugglers, tramps and vagabonds.

Some of them loved the place so much that they never left. Their spirits wander here. A headless man roamed the Ridge, another one with a hat haunted the road leading to Annadale. An English woman in a white bridal dress is seen on the Mall and the Ridge. Oh, there used to be so many ghosts! Where are they now, wondered Malkiat.

It seems that they did not like the development activities of Shimla. Old buildings have been destroyed in fire making the ghosts homeless, Malkiat thought. They must have migrated to the interiors of the Shimla hills or left for some new place, he mused.

ঔ

'Dadaji, tell me the story,' Deepa interrupted his thoughts.

'Hmm, I will tell you about the ghosts of Shimla.'

'Ghosts!' Her eyes widened. 'Are you serious, Dadaji?' she whispered.

'You go and play, I need time to think,' he said.

'For how long? When should I come?' the child asked.

'Half an hour; run fast! If you say another word I will not tell you anything,' he said with mock anger and was lost in his thoughts as the child disappeared.

ঔ

Malkiat recalled that Shimla has always had its share of unexplained mysteries. One such character was Jacob.

AM Jacob, who surprised many, arrived in Shimla in 1871. Who was he and from where he emerged, remained a mystery. Some said he was Persian and his real name was Abdul Hafiz Bin Isak. The secret department of the British government had a dossier on him as he was believed to be a Russian spy. He was fluent in English, Turkish, Persian, Urdu, Arabic and French. He fascinated writers like no one else. Rudyard Kipling immortalized him as Lurgan Sahib in *Kim*, Francis Marion Crawford described him in *Mr Isaacs: A Tale of Modern India*, and Colonel Davis recognized him as Emanuel in his novel, *Jadoo*.

Jacob would turn invisible amidst an audience! When invited to parties he would often suddenly disappear from the table, but people could see his fork and spoon work on the dishes! Shocked guests saw an invisible entity gulping food! Weak hearts fainted and many avoided his company. He told one of his lady friends that he was gifted these miraculous powers by a pir who lived for six hundred years.

ꕥ

'Dadaji? Dadaji?'

Malkiat opened his eyes reluctantly and saw Deepa standing a few feet away staring at him.

'Dadaji, are you sleeping?' she asked.

'I wasn't sleeping, I was thinking,' he said groggily.

'Now run away, it will take me another half hour, but come at the exact time, not early.'

The child ran away, she was losing faith in Dadaji's ability to tell her about Shimla. He didn't even know how many years he had lived!

ଓ

Malkiat closed his eyes again. Shimla had so many haunted houses. Edward J. Buck has recorded ghostly houses in his legendary work, *Shimla: Past and Present*. Colonel TD Colyear, who owned many houses in Shimla, had a special connection with the ghosts. One of his houses was known as 'The Alice Bower'. It was haunted by the ghost of Alice, his second wife. After his death the property devolved to Alice and her relatives came to stay with her. When she died, her apparition haunted the house for some time before disappearing forever. The story of his first wife, a native Muslim lady, is no less strange. When she died in 1875, she was buried in the compound of Juba House located on the way to Bishop Cotton School. After the colonel's death, Juba House was sold and the new owner objected to a grave in the compound. So the grave was dug up in the presence of the deputy commissioner, a representative of the family, a solicitor, a police officer, a civil surgeon and a few friends. Her remains were coffined again and she was buried in the cemetery. A garden was raised on the site of her grave.

Oh, there are so many bizarre tales in Shimla, thought Malkiat Singh, and a chill ran down his spine as he remembered his encounter with the ghost.

ᘓ

'Are you sleeping again, Dadaji?'

Malkiat heard the small, tentative voice and panicked. 'No, I am not sleeping...still thinking,' he said sheepishly.

'What are you thinking about?'

'The ghost of the mansion,' he blurted out.

'Tell me its story,' she said excitedly.

'Okay, I will write about it. You come again after some time,' said Malkiat Singh, dismissing the child and went down the memory lane again.

In those years, he had developed the habit of going for an after-dinner walk on the Ridge. When he met an old friend of his who took him to his house located on the way to the Jakhoo temple. Hours passed chatting and recollecting old memories. It was nearly midnight when Malkiat left his friend's house.

Soon he reached the mansion shining majestically in the moonlight. He stopped for a while to admire the beautiful house with immaculate greens. Suddenly he heard voices from behind him. Curious to know who would be there so late, he turned back. There were two Englishmen, dressed in military uniform, conversing in soft voices with each other. He stared at them, surprised, and wanted to know who they were, when both of them turned and started to walk towards the mansion. Before he could utter a word they had crossed the barbed fence of the house as if it did not exist, and had entered the greens!

Scared and wondering what was happening, he sneaked at them in the garden. They walked towards the porch and sat on a wrought-iron bench nearby. He could see both of them smoking and chatting animatedly. Maybe they were guests in the house, he thought for a moment, but remembered how they had passed through the barbed fence. He looked away and then again towards the porch and was astounded to find that no one was there! They had vanished into thin air. Malkiat stood there for some time, speechless, and then walked away to his house quickly.

The next day he told his wife about the incident who laughed at him and he forgot about it till he met his friend again. When he mentioned it to him, his friend was surprised. The mansion had been lying unoccupied for nearly two years! Moreover, his friend told him that there was something spooky about the mansion. Many people had seen the two ghosts in full army uniform wandering in and around the garden or sitting on the bench near the porch, chatting and smoking!

There was no doubt he too had seen the two ghosts that night!

'Dadaji, have you written anything?' Deepa was now exasperated.

'I will write, give me some time.'

'No, return my notebook, I will find some other old man. You know nothing. You don't even know how long you have lived,' the child said accusingly and ran away picking up the notebook from his lap.

'Nothing?' He smiled. He was known as the most authoritative scholar on the colonial history of Shimla. He smiled again and closed his eyes.

The Possessed

'Meat *lao, sharab lao. Abhi lao*,' the voice spat with vengeance.

There were three of us apart from the victim—her mother, her brother and I, a neighbour. This drama had been going on for nearly three weeks, every evening at the same time: 5.45 p.m. And the victim was a frail, fourteen year-old girl!

Her elder brother and I, a body builder, were trying to hold her writhing and jerking body down. She weighed a mere forty kilograms! The strength she possessed boggled me on the first day it happened, but we were getting used to this spirit taking over her body. Today he was very angry and wanted to destroy her.

Acquainted with him now, I had even started chatting up with the spirit. As I tried to pin her legs down on the bed, I asked in a harsh voice, 'Why do you keep troubling her? Why don't you go away?' I was anxious, wondering how long this would go on. I wanted to go back and play cricket with my college friends, but every evening I had to be home for this long-dead man. 'That's what neighbours are for!' my mother would often say.

'Give me something to eat and drink, meat *aur sharab*...I will not leave her,' said the spirit angrily as froth and spittle flew from the victim's mouth. It was not the girl's voice. She had such a soft and sweet voice. But when this 'character' entered her, her voice would turn hoarse and growly. I was exasperated, not scared anymore.

We had all accepted the fact that a dead man's spirit entered her every evening. This timid, frail girl looked so grotesque and different from her usual self—eyes red with anger and hatred, her mouth curled up, sneering at us mere mortals. She was a small but beautiful girl with curious eyes. How a calm and pleasant girl turned into a scary demon was a wonder. Moreover, her body became so powerful that twice she had thrown me off and once I was flung off, hitting the door and landing on the ground. I was flabbergasted by her, or should I say, 'his' strength!

In fact, a part of me wanted to compete with that strength and I began to practise muscle exercises. I did weight-lifting and push-ups regularly, knowing I had to fight him in the evening!

Now I cursed him loudly—we had got used to harsh language—and repeated, 'Get out of her or I will kill you.' He started laughing. Not the roaring laugh but the shrieking ominous laugh which gave you goosebumps.

'Who are you, little boy, to order me like that? What if I leave her and enter your body,' he said and broke into a spine-chilling giggle. Surprised, I let go of one of the legs, and got a resounding smack from him as I reached for that leg again. I will knock him out, I thought. 'So you want to come inside me? Come...' I shouted. I could hear aunty, the girl's mother, whimpering near the door. That was all she did whenever her daughter went into this state.

His laugh, I can't lie, scared me to death. But then wasn't I a macho man? I had to fight back. 'I am ready; leave this girl and come into me. I will set you right,' I hastily added like a fool. Her brother, clutching her hands, stared at me in awe, I felt him hero-worship me and this boosted my courage. The spirit then repeated, 'I want sharab...get me meat.'

ര

As I sit here near the same spot after twenty-seven years, I am sceptical. Did all that really happen? Everything has changed since then. There used to be only a few houses below Oak Over behind Lady Reading Hospital at that time. Now there's a haphazard jungle of concrete with houses cluttering the area in such a way that you don't know which door belonged to which house. I went down and tried to locate where our old house had stood, but in vain.

Now there are four-storey buildings all around and the ambience of the place has changed, too. Probably everything changes with time. I watch the chaatwallah selling chaat to a group of three school children who are Port More School girls. Port More was the school in which she had studied. Where was she now?

Port More was the happening girls' school of Shimla at that time. She had to walk through the graveyard located between our houses and the school every day. She had been doing this for so many years, but till then nothing had happened. The spirit had entered her body in this graveyard, that man had said this himself. But why it entered into her is a mystery. The spirit never explained that.

According to her family, the girl had urinated on one of the graves one afternoon during the school break as the sun blazed through the branches of the lofty deodars. I do not know if it was an offhand remark, as far as I remember, because the girl never mentioned it. After the spirit would leave her, the poor thing would not remember anything about what had happened to her. Moreover, she would be too exhausted to talk about it. But then I wasn't one of the family, I was just a neighbour, a boy living next door.

As I brood about bygone times, I notice that the rain shelter is still intact though it has got a new roof, new walls and fresh paint. And not for a moment is there any slowdown in the vehicular traffic on this so-called Sealed Road. Vehicles are zipping past non-stop, red light or no red light. Where is the spirit now, I wonder, and how does it feel about this modernization?

ᴥ

'I am extremely angry,' said the spirit.

I retorted, 'I too feel very angry.' Sweat drops glistened on my forehead when I pinned her down on the bed to stop her from hurting herself or me as she writhed vengefully.

My mother had told me not to speak with the spirit, but I was not in the mood to adhere to her advice. I mean if 'he' had no problem talking, I could do the same. So ignoring all my mother's advice I snapped back, 'Why are you so angry?'

'I have suffered a lot,' replied the spirit, but this time in a wailing tone. There was no anger in his voice. Surprisingly, I sympathized with him. This was all so crazy. Imagine an eighteen-year-old boy pitying a spirit! 'But why are you troubling this poor girl? What is her fault?' I said firmly. This is not justice, what has she got to do with his suffering? I thought.

The spirit repeated, 'I have suffered a lot.' He loved repeating himself and that frustrated me.

'I am not a thief...I never wanted to be one,' the spirit said out of the blue.

Really? This was interesting. What did he mean? This was for the first time that he had said something that gave some insight into what motivated his behaviour. We waited so as not to goad him. He went silent and then left the girl's body, like on other days.

☙

How engrossed I had become then! Well, it was an engrossing experience for a young boy.

There was some mystery to be solved, I thought amusedly, at that time. The next day, in fact, I waited for my mother to tell me to go to the neighbouring house. I wanted to go there and talk to the spirit instead of playing cricket. Imagine I was willing to sacrifice my play time for that unfinished conversation! It was the twenty-sixth day.

There was a different atmosphere in the room; even aunty and her brother tried to ignore me. They were neither rude nor hospitable, but indifferent. I wanted to talk to the spirit.

'I am not a thief,' it repeated, to my sheer delight, as we wrestled with him.

'Then who are you?'

'I was innocent.' I was deflated. That is what all the guilty say, there was going to be nothing new, I thought in frustration. But what the spirit said further still rings in my ears, especially at night. His voice—full of misery and despair—is something I can never forget. There was helplessness and a plea for us to understand him.

'I was made a thief forcibly. The white man committed the robbery but I was made the culprit. What could I do... no one listened to my pleas. No one accepted me after that. I was left with no option. My family disowned me. I had to kill myself in the end. But I could not rest in peace. '

'So stop troubling the poor girl, it is not her fault,' I said.

'I need someone to speak through. I want my story to be told. And maybe you will help me in getting mukti.'

'How will you get mukti?' I asked.

'How would I know,' he growled and went silent.

That was the last time I had a conversation with the spirit. From what the spirit revealed, it appeared that the man was made scapegoat for a robbery committed by a British man. The same evening I was told by aunty that there was no need to come, it was beyond them to handle the situation and her brother—the girl's mama—had called someone from a village near their ancestral place who knew how to handle these supernatural beings.

ca

I was somewhat disappointed that day but in a few days, things became normal. Something really did happen there.

Now, as the sun sets through the deodars, I recall those words and wonder whether the poor thing is in peace. Or the spirit is still hovering somewhere here, entering someone else's body to gain mukti.

The Knock

'If you are looking for ghosts, there is one place where you may confirm their presence—the Charabra Helipad,' thirty-year-old Devesh stated dramatically.

I was a little sceptical. Though I had been to the helipad a number of times, I had never heard about it being haunted. It is located at a distance of about ten kilometres from Shimla. The helipad is basically for the president's helicopter and those of other VVIPs. For the rest of the time, it is a tourist place buzzing with yak rides, tea stalls, momo stalls and chaatwallahs catering to the tourists who come to see the beautiful views from the flat ridge.

The field of vision is 360 degrees and exhibits one of the most majestic landscapes of the Shimla hills—the

Great Himalayan ranges to the north and northwest, a lush green carpet of thick forest locally known as Hussan Valley on the eastern side, the expanding Shimla outskirts on the western side, the Kufri expanse on the northern side and rolling green hills towards the south.

On the outskirts before you reach the helipad, lies one of the oldest schools—Himalayan International School. In front of the helipad, after a couple of hillocks, is President's Retreat.

Devesh's anecdote was spine-chilling. He had gone to the helipad late one evening along with three friends. On their way back from Rampur, they had decided to go to the helipad to watch the twinkling lights of Shimla. The ground was empty with no tourists or locals.

They got out of the car and stretched for a little while, but the cold and the silence forced them to take refuge in the car again. They were discussing the power of mother nature, when suddenly there was a knock on the car window! A clear and loud knock. It was dark outside and no one was visible from inside the car.

Before any of them could say a single word there was another knock, this time louder. Each one of them could sense the other's terror. Uneasiness settled on them. They also heard voices and conversation in hushed tones! Devesh was on the driver's seat. With trembling hands, he started the car and drove down in maximum speed to the main road. Once he reached there, he stopped to catch his breath. They looked at each other—all of them were terror-struck and unable to speak. They had heard that knock. When they were strolling a few minutes earlier on the helipad, they had not seen anyone! Who could it be then? Certainly, it was no human being. Same with the voices they had heard, knowing clearly that there was no one around!

ଊ

So I decided to investigate. Not only because it was a spooky tale, but also because the helipad is a fetching place, one of my favourites. I went there with a few friends. It had snowed just two days back. Our car could not go beyond Charabra Bazaar. No problem, we decided to walk and it was great fun.

Stomping on the snow, our first walk this winter! I asked the people I met on the way if this place was haunted. Some shrugged in the negative, while others stated that they had heard strange tales—the small hillock beyond the helipad was said to be haunted. But there was no definitive answer to my queries.

There was no one on the helipad except for a couple clicking photographs of each other. We strolled on the helipad discussing ghosts, enjoying the wide expanse of virgin beauty. As we were returning to the bazaar, I saw three boys sitting on the pavement nearby. I stopped and unabashedly asked them whether they were locals or tourists.

The boys were locals. I introduced myself and told them about my mission to confirm Devesh's encounter. The youngsters were not forthcoming at first, but soon they opened up and said that they had never seen the ghost but had heard stories about the hillock beyond the helipad. They further told me that there was another place nearby which was haunted, just opposite Charabra Bazaar where a link road goes to a high-end hotel. On this small link road comes a stretch where people have experienced the supernatural.

I was intrigued and asked them, 'What happens there?'

'You can hear both male and female voices of people talking near you, but you can't see anyone. The headlights of vehicles start to flicker on their own, on-off-on-off... No one ventures out there all alone.'

I was satisfied, at least I got some information. Thanking them and forgetting about the ghosts, I decided to concentrate on the slippery climb down the snow-covered road. When we touched the main road that goes to the Retreat, the summer house of the president of India, we stopped to glance at Priyanka Gandhi's house, which was under construction. Here I met another young man walking on the road and asked him the same question. He was an employee working at the Retreat.

He related two incidents he had heard about, which happened at a time when there was no electricity and the population was sparse. One of his senior colleagues had narrated this experience to him. Many years ago when he was going to the Retreat alone at night, he encountered a ghost! When he reached the big curve on the road to the Retreat, he sensed that he was not alone. He hoped it was someone from the Retreat, but all he could make out was a blurred figure, manlike. He also told himself that he might be hallucinating, but he was not drunk and could clearly see the strange figure now walk ahead of him.

It was a dark moonless night. First, he thought of calling out to the stranger, but then changed his mind and decided to light a matchstick to see who was there. He saw no one when he lit the matchstick! When the flame died he saw the man again, now lingering close to him. This happened a few more times, after which he was convinced it was a spirit. He also knew it was not harmful, otherwise he would have been attacked and killed by then.

Though he was frightened, he kept walking hurriedly, mumbling a prayer. He heaved a sigh of relief when he reached the gate of the Retreat. On entering the campus he turned around, there was no one on the road. He was all alone!

The second story related by the young man was told to him by his grandfather. 'My grandfather lived in a small village near Thaila below Mashobra. He was a farmer and grew vegetables. He, along with other farmers, would sell their vegetables in Shimla Sabzi Mandi. Since they had to reach Shimla by 6 a.m., they would leave their village after midnight and walk with their produce—cabbage, peas, cauliflowers, beans and tomatoes.

'The group had to walk in the dead of night for there were no buses or vehicles plying at that time. Carrying vegetables in the kiltas, they would reach the Sipur ground, where an annual fair is held even now. Sipur fair is famous for bullfights. Between Mashobra and Fairlawns, there was a steep *dhank* (gorge) near which was a *kud* (a natural cave shelter), where they rested and waited for the day to break before they started on the next leg of their journey. From Mashobra till they reached the cave shelter, a chudail always accompanied them and sat alongside them quietly. No one talked to her but everyone was aware of her presence. With the first rays of sun out, they moved on further to Shimla leaving the chudail behind. She was their constant companion night after night till the kud!'

ଔ

Now it was my turn to narrate spooky tales to Devesh!

Believe it or Not

Raj looked out of the window. It was nature's glorious painting. The sun had risen, its orange-yellow luminosity atop the snow-peaked mountains, its golden rays spreading sparkle all over. Its warmth had not yet hugged the region, however, and the chill in the air made him close the window. He watched the scene through the glass in the warmth of his room where a bukhari was hissing and fizzing with a life of its own. It was a cozy setting. It was his third day here in the bounty of nature, but sadly even this heavenly bliss could not lift the cloud of gloom that had settled upon him. In fact he was here on a mission, to investigate his best friend's strange condition.

Raj had five more days left to find the truth and, if possible, search for a cure as well. Every time he wanted to inhale the fresh air, feast his eyes on the white-peaked mountains and go for long leisurely walks in the thick woods heavy with the sweet fragrance of pines, his mind drifted to Ajay, his friend who had lost everything in these very hills.

He wondered what must have happened. A polite bang on the door interrupted his thoughts.

'Good morning, sir, did you have sweet dreams? Hope it was not too cold...you should have drawn the curtains. I see the boy has already lit the bukhari, but don't ever draw away these curtains. They are thick and specially designed to keep away the cold.' The endless chatter of Gopal, the all-in-one caretaker of the lodge, left him irritated but Raj needed his help.

Gopal was so many things rolled into one—waiter, gardener, cook and caretaker of the lodge. He would minutely scrutinize the room every time he entered, throw some advice at him, and then spoke non-stop about his favourite topic—the hill people were not fools to be duped by one and all. He would boast about visiting big cities like Delhi, Bombay, Lucknow and Allahabad. He had made loads of money there and no one had the guts to act smart with him, since all the goondas of the area were his friends!

'When I had gone to Bombay last year, I saw the tall actress Shilpa Shetty,' he said today while drawing back the window curtains. It was for the first time that the little devil had mentioned a Bollywood star; he was full of surprises.

'Really, that must have been very exciting. Was she good-looking?' Raj asked.

'Not really, I don't approve of the things they smear on their faces, they look more like bandariyas! The clothes they wear...' and then he whistled loudly.

'Anyone would look tantalizing in them,' Raj helped him finish the sentence. He was not sure whether Gopal was bluffing or had actually seen the actress.

'Our paharans, sir, their beauty is unmatchable and if they dress like the ones in Bombay, they will look like angels,' the boy said.

'Yes. They have a natural beauty, ivory-coloured skin with pink cheeks, they sure are pretty.'

'Hmm...however, may I remind you that our girls know how to take care of themselves. They are smart, so you cannot play games with them,' he said in a threatening tone.

'Of course, nowadays you cannot play games with anyone, young man. And don't you worry, I have no intention of mixing with your hill women. Now tell me what have you made for breakfast. I will be down in a few minutes after taking my bath,' Raj said, dismissing the boy.

ଔ

Raj worked as a senior executive in a multinational company based in Delhi. His friends Ajay and Lakshay had come here last year on a holiday. They were found unconscious in the forest near Narkanda. Ajay could not survive, whereas Lakshay had been in a delirium since then. All treatment had failed to cure him. Sometimes he talked about a spirit that had attacked them in the forest. Since someone had suggested that the locals of the area would know the cause and the cure, Raj decided to travel to Narkanda.

He took a bus to Shimla. This was his first visit. He could feel the freshness in the air upon entering Himachal at Parwanoo. When he stepped down from the bus in Shimla near Victory Tunnel, he was surrounded by a group of eight to ten Kashmiri khans who grabbed and pushed him in different directions, and to his bewilderment, he saw his luggage being carried away by one of the Khans while he was being taken in the opposite direction!

Thankfully, a policeman intervened. Late in the evening he had ultimately landed in a hotel room, dingy and windowless, but in one piece along with his luggage. The next day while he was going to the Tourist Information Centre on Mall Road, he was swarmed by the so-called travel agents and guides offering him sight-seeing trips. He managed to enter the information centre with some difficulty. There he booked a taxi for Narkanda.

He decided to stay at Hill View, a small lodge near the bus stand. His room had a panoramic view of ridges where small hamlets were perched.

ᘛ

'Where do you plan to go today?' asked the boy as Raj came with his breakfast.

'Hmm...maybe I will take the same path I took yesterday. Today you must call that pandit you were talking about. I don't have much time left,' Raj said.

'Yes, I think he will come today. He had gone away to perform a special puja. He knows a lot and will tell you everything. But I suggest you don't venture out into the forest alone, you won't find anything. Also, it can be dangerous.'

Raj was worried, but determined to know the truth. For three days he visited several small villages around Narkanda to enquire about the spirits haunting the jungles. He heard many strange tales and many people confirmed that there were ghosts and spirits in the forest, but they did not normally disturb humans.

Most villagers knew about the accident that had happened with his friends. Both of them were found unconscious in the forest by local people. They must have remained there for the entire night because their bodies were numb. While one of them could be revived, the other was declared dead by the doctors. Everyone agreed that it was an attack by the spirits, and said that the boys must have annoyed the local spirits by drinking near their sacred abode.

He was spellbound when they told him about the practice of *mashania*. They said that some selected people who had attained siddhi could call back the dead and talk to them to ascertain the cause of their death. But they needed some personal belonging of the dead person to call the spirit. Initially he found all this ridiculous, but three days here in this part of the world had led him to believe otherwise. The villagers also told him about Pandit Keval Ram Kashyap who could call the spirits, but right now he was in a remote village performing sacred rituals and no one could tell when he would be back. There was no way to contact him. No mobiles or landlines worked where he had gone. Raj decided to wait.

Every day he would roam the forests around Narkanda in search of clues to the bizarre incident that had led to the death of his friend, but found nothing. Did ghosts and spirits exist at all? How could someone call back the dead and talk to them? Was it right for him to get into all this? But he wanted to know the truth. He had already asked his friends in Delhi to courier some of Ajay's personal belongings.

Raj completed another fruitless walk in the forest without finding witches or ghosts, and returned to the hotel. He was hungry. When he reached the hotel the cheerful Gopal informed him that Panditji had returned and was waiting for him. His hunger vanished.

Panditji was a pleasant-looking man. He was old but very fit and alert. He gave Raj a warm and affectionate smile. Raj instantly thought that this man could never lie.

'Tell me, son, what brings you here?' asked Panditji. Raj was moved and, on an impulse, touched his feet and explained to him his reason behind coming to Narkanda. Raj also told him that every day he wandered in the forest to find out what had happened to his friends.

Panditji smiled compassionately and was not mocking Raj when he said, 'You don't meet these creatures every day. They have a special time when they come out of hiding. Your friends must have done something really silly to annoy them. You have come at the right time. The day after tomorrow I will be calling spirits. You know, this cannot be done every day. So, come to my house in the evening at about seven, by that time most other people would have left.

'Do not forget to bring a personal belonging of your friend—maybe a cloth worn by him, his handkerchief, a diary or a pen. Anything will do. It should have been used by him for a reasonable amount of time. Gopal will bring you to my house. Don't worry. No one dies before their time, so do not grieve for your friend. His life might have been short.'

Panditji left. Raj was anxious; the courier had not arrived and there was not much time left, so he called his friends in Delhi and asked one of them to start immediately for Narkanda with the personal belongings of Ajay. He spent a restless night full of nightmares about demons and evil spirits. He woke up many times in fear, but then remembered the smiling face of Panditji and felt peaceful and calm again.

The next day he did not go anywhere and stayed in his room. His friend Mohit arrived from Delhi with some clothes and a diary of Ajay by the evening. Mohit wanted to know everything, so Raj briefed him. He also told him about the witch that haunted the forest. 'She takes you with her to the nearby running stream and then reveals several different forms of herself. She looks normal but her feet are turned backwards.'

'Have you met her?' asked Mohit.

'No, but I believe in all this after coming here,' said Raj.

'You are getting paranoid. But let us see this spirit-calling business tomorrow, then everything will become clear. Though I feel this is just nonsense,' said Mohit.

'Don't say that. We must not jump to conclusions. There are so many unexplained things in nature,' Raj tried to convince Mohit.

ଔ

The next day, they went to Panditji's house. Gopal told them that Panditji called the spirits of the dead and talked to them once every fifteen days. He was so popular that people came from far and away to meet him and there was a token system. People came a day in advance and waited for their turn. Gopal was right—they saw several cars with number plates from Punjab, Haryana and Delhi, moving uphill from Panditji's village.

'They have all come to clear their doubts,' said Gopal.

Mohit wanted to stop some of them and ask them about their experience, but Raj did not allow him. In about half an hour they reached Panditji's house. They were received by his son who entered their address in a register and asked them to wait.

After fifteen minutes they were called inside. In an empty room they were told to take their shoes off, wash their hands and feet, and cover their heads with a white cloth. Then they entered another room. Both of them were scared. It was a small room where lots of dhoop and agarbattis had made the room hazy. Whatever light there was emerged from a small jyot in one corner. Panditji's son gestured them to sit on a carpet. Suddenly they saw a shrouded figure in the corner near the jyot and shuddered. They looked at Panditji's son and he signalled them to keep quiet by putting his fingers to his lips. He left Ajay's belongings near the shrouded figure and left the room.

Both Raj and Mohit sat there speechless, waiting for something to happen. A hand emerged from the white shroud and the clothes of Ajay were dragged inside. There was silence for some time and then a deep throaty voice came from the corner, 'What do you want to know?'

It was scary. For a few moments both of them could

not speak. Raj recognized the voice to be Panditji's and stammered, 'We...what happened to him?'

Then there was silence again. They could make out some muffled chanting. They did not know what to do when suddenly the room was filled with cries and howls. Both Raj and Mohit screamed in fear, they wanted to run out of the room but their feet froze. Slowly the screams died and they heard a clear voice, 'Do not grieve for me. My life was to end this way only. In my previous birth I had committed a sin and I got what I deserved. Tell my family that I am happy and secure.'

It was amazing that both the friends recognized Ajay's voice. There was no doubt it was Ajay. How could that be? They were trying to comprehend the full meaning of what was happening when they heard another voice. This time it was Panditji, 'Ask him what you want, he will not stay on for long.'

Shivering with fear Raj said, 'What had happened to you?'

'No use in knowing that, my friend,' the voice said, 'just remember, this was destiny. But do not ever mock the spirits and ghosts. They are as real as you and me. Take some soil and water from the stream where we were found for Lakshya, he will be all right. Tell my family not to worry.'

There was silence, and then the room was filled with screams and cries again. After a while, these sounds vanished and an eerie stillness filled the room. Both the friends sat there speechless and motionless for some time. Then they saw the shroud move and Ajay's clothes were flung towards them. Panditji gestured them to leave. They got up on ginger feet and moved out slowly, clasping each other's hands.

They came out and collapsed on the mat in the room. Gopal gave them water to drink. It took them some time to bring their breath back to normal. They were scared and dread filled their hearts. But what they had experienced was real. After some time Raj expressed his desire to meet Panditji, but his son said that they could see him only in the morning, and that there were other people waiting. Moreover, Panditji was exhausted after the gruelling schedule and did not meet anyone.

The next morning the two of them accompanied Gopal to bring water and soil from the place where Ajay and Lakshya were found. Later in the day they met Panditji again who told them to smear the soil on the forehead of Lakshya and to give him spring water to drink.

Reaching Delhi, they did as told by Panditji. Lakshya had a miraculous recovery in two months. What more proof was needed!

Bhoot Bangla, Tea Party and Fairies

The life of Mr Raman Chabra, a retired officer of the Indian Institute of Advanced Studies (IIAS), is extraordinary. Most of his family members claim paranormal experiences. They have not only met ghosts and spirits but have walked beside them, fought with them, threatened them and have seen fairies land and fly away to the world they belong.

When he joined the IIAS in the late '60s, Mr Chabra was allotted Room No. 6. He moved immediately into his new home with his wife. The building was officially named Karainchi Lane, but was also known as Bhoot Bangla. However, when he occupied the residence he had no idea what it was called. The building had two dozen single rooms with one bathroom for every four rooms. It was on the north-facing slope in a thick grove of oak and

Kail trees, with the sun caressing it barely for an hour or so. It was a cold and desolate place, not preferred by the employees of the institute. But it was not a bad place as first allotment.

☙

That fateful night they had their supper at 7 o'clock in the evening. Though it was a one-room accommodation, the couple spent hours discussing how they would arrange furniture in their room. Suddenly they heard a raucous noise, as if a number of people were walking outside the room on the balcony and talking loudly.

Mr Chabra was irritated. His wife advised him to ignore the people outside—maybe they were drunkards—but he couldn't help himself. He was angry that this group was being so disruptive; he ignored his wife's pleas and flung the door open to reprimand them. To his utter amazement there was no one outside! It was so quiet he could hear his own breathing.

And then he had a strange sensation. He felt as if someone was drawing out his strength, the very essence of his life was being drained, not through his heart but through his brain; his soul was being sucked! Then he felt a tremendous pain in his chest; he screamed as loudly as he could.

His wife came running to him and when she saw his pale face, distorted in pain, she screamed too. Their screams woke the neighbours up who then came to help. He was, by now, drained of all energy, trembling uncontrollably, though the pain in his chest had subsided. Neighbours gave him all kinds of home remedies for nearly two hours, but he did not feel better. Whenever his gaze travelled towards the door he felt a chill.

At last the neighbours left, but he could not sleep. He felt restless, and eventually woke his wife up telling her that he wanted to go to the toilet. She decided to accompany him. He felt strange, but had not imagined what awaited him outside the door.

Just as he put one foot on to the balcony, something invisible seized his body and threw him back into the room; it was sheer luck that his head had not hit any pointed or hard thing. His wife was also lifted up and thrown out into the balcony. Their screams of terror woke the neighbours up again and they came rushing. They picked the terrified couple up and carried them to their beds. People were surprised and wanted to know what had happened, but they were in no condition to recount their ordeal.

Mr Chabra realized that this was the work of an evil spirit which wanted to harm them. Concentrating hard, he prayed to his kul devta. The spirit struck again and the invisible force picked him up from the bed and flung him back on to the floor. Everyone was horrified by this sight. After that he did not recall anything until next morning.

His brother who lived near Mall Road was summoned. He came along with a doctor. The doctor could not find anything wrong and concluded that it probably was indigestion!

But Mr Chabra could make out that the cause lay elsewhere. He knew of a cobbler from Kangra who had the powers to handle evil spirits and wandering phantoms. The next day he, along with his wife, went to see this cobbler who worked in a shack on the way to Lal Pani School below the bus stand. They explained to him what had happened.

The cobbler took a coin out, babbled some mantras and then threw the coin on a *sil* (a stone slab for grinding), after which he studied its position and made some calculations. He announced that the power of his kul devta and Chabra's own courage had saved their lives. There were several spirits in the building. He said that the women living in that building would always be unwell. Mr Chabra later found out that his female neighbours would perpetually feel tired, energyless and unhealthy.

The cobbler then performed a special ritual and gave them about two fistfuls of mustard seeds with magical powers, to be thrown within a radius of one kilometre in the area at 12 o'clock on a moonless night; no one should see them doing this. The cobbler also warned them, 'The evil spirits would attack someone in the building at least one more time, but you will have to be brave to face their wrath. No fatal harm will come to you. After that there will be no more attacks.'

So on the coming Amavasya, Mr Chabra went into the thick jungle alone and scattered the mustard seeds. He awaited the forthcoming attack apprehensively. As the week approached the end, he became less jittery but the unfortunate incident happened .

Their immediate neighbour's younger brother was visiting for a few days. He had the habit of going to the toilet more than once in the night. On the last day of his stay when he ventured out of the room, he was picked up and thrown down into the forest in the dead of the night. No one heard his screams for help. The next morning he was discovered by the rescue party in the jungle below the building. He remained unconscious for two days. Luckily he survived with minor scratches.

This time everyone was terrified. The neighbours finally told Mr Chabra that strange things happened there frequently and that is why this annex was known as Bhoot Bangla. Mr Chabra was not worried; he knew that nothing bad would happen since proper measures had been taken.

Later, the building was reconstructed to make two-room apartments. Thankfully, there is nothing to fear and very few people know that a Bhoot Bangla stood here five decades ago.

ঙ

Another interesting story is that of a carpenter from Kanlog area narrated by Mr Chabra's brother-in-law.

One evening, the carpenter had been working on a piece of wood, when the oil lamp flickered and a strange fragrance suddenly filled the room. He looked towards the door on a reflex. To his surprise he saw an Englishman standing on the threshold of the open door. But what struck him as odd about the Englishman was that he looked hazy—more of a silhouette than a real man—he rubbed his eyes thinking that perhaps his eyesight was failing, but, no, the figure was still hazy. The carpenter felt his heart tighten as he realized that the visitor was not a human being, but a ghost. The spirit must have come from the nearby cemetery. He started trembling in the fear of what would happen to him.

To his astonishment, the spirit demanded a cup of tea! He thought he had not heard it right but the ghost reiterated the demand again, 'I want tea and bread.' He spoke in Hindi! All the carpenter could mumble was, 'I don't have milk to prepare tea,' to which the spirit replied, 'I will come tomorrow. Give it to me then,' and disappeared in front of his eyes.

The poor fellow was panic-stricken and in a dilemma about what to do. He thought of leaving home but had no other place to go. With the meagre money he had, he bought some milk, a small packet of bread and a few biscuits the following day. Never before had he bought biscuits and bread, he was too poor to afford such luxuries.

Around the same time in the evening he made tea, laid the table and waited in anticipation. When he started feeling uneasy, he hid himself beneath the bed and waited with baited breath for the ghost. It entered the room, drank tea, ate the snacks he had brought, and then left the room without uttering a single word.

For a long time the carpenter did not have the courage to come out from under the bed. It was only when his body could not bear the cold and discomfort that he came out of his hiding place. He was still in shock when, to his astonishment, he found an old bag on the table. It was definitely not his, oh God! The ghost had forgotten his things and would now come again. He had no money to buy milk and bread for him, he thought in despair.

He could not sleep a wink and kept staring at the bag. He trembled with fear and cried at his fate. The next morning he mustered the courage to open the bag. He could not believe his eyes when he saw the contents of the bag. The bag was full of glittering gold and jewellery. This was a treasure. He was intrigued—where had the spirit brought this from and why had he left it here at his home! Had he forgotten it? Would he come again? For a week he waited for the Englishman to come for his treasure.

And then one night the spirit visited him in his dream and said, 'This treasure is yours, I have given it to you.' That is how the poor carpenter became one of the richest men of Shimla. The excited carpenter narrated this unbelievable tale to the neighbours. A few others also tried to woo the spirit to come to their house by leaving the door open and laying a table with bread, biscuits and tea. But all in vain!

ঞ

Mr Chabra narrated these strange tales to me in the lawns of IIAS where I met him. He concluded his stories with this one.

'Why do you think the training institute of the health department in Shimla is known as Pari Mehal? My mother and my aunt had seen small bright specks coming down from the sky. They danced here in front of the building, and after some time went back into the sky to mingle with the stars on the horizon. These were spirits with wings who flew down to enjoy themselves and party, after which they returned to their abode high up in the sky. The place where they landed and flew away from was known as Pari Mehal.'

And then he added, 'My sister has fed ghosts. A chudail followed my jijaji while he was returning home late in the night in Bemloe area. My brother was also followed by a ghost on the Ridge.'

ঞ

Oh, what a strange family!

The Road Hunters

Girish Hosur, from Karnataka, was an officer in the forest department. Together, we had planned a holiday to Kinnaur. When we reached Kufri, the driver stopped the vehicle at a temple before a blind curve to pay obeisance to the local diety.

'Why are there temples on so many curves in Himachal, especially on the trickiest ones?' Girish asked. I shrugged. I had no idea. 'Maybe you haven't noticed, but they are located at every loop and bend on the roads,' he insisted.

Rakesh, my husband, replied lightly, 'You better choose one for yourself.'

'What! A temple, I don't understand,' he said.

'No, a curve! These are places where there have been accidents and people have built temples in the memory of the dead,' Rakesh said in mock seriousness. 'That is why I am asking you to select a picturesque spot for yourself. One is always travelling on such narrow roads.'

'Yes, yes, I got it,' Girish said, a little shaken. 'This is scary but I am not interested in any bend or curve. I want to return safely to Karnataka to my family,' he added firmly. We all laughed it off as we moved ahead.

'The sites where people die in accidents become haunted, because the spirits of the dead scout the area. Since these are accident-prone places anyway, temples are constructed here in order to please these restless souls,' the driver explained to us, the non-believers.

'This may be a superstition or the hallucination of tired drivers,' Girish quipped.

The driver, a young boy in his twenties, shook his head, 'No, sir, these are neither hallucinations nor superstitions. These are things that are seen and felt. So many drivers report sightings of supernatural beings. We believe in this: that is why whenever we buy a new vehicle we pray to Goddess Kali and keep a picture of her with us.'

'Are you afraid to drive at night?' Girish asked, his curiosity aroused.

'Yes, but we have our own ways of handling such situations. We carry trishuls, chant or spit at some places. Some drivers light a matchstick before crossing a particular spot, and then throw it away on the road,' he said matter-of-factly.

'Some keep magic seeds in the vehicle. These can be bought from a man near Solan to keep evil spirits away. We have our own favourite temples on selected routes where we pray and the gods protect us,' he added, as we exchanged glances.

As the vehicle sped by, another temple appeared near Theog and then another one a little ahead. I began to wonder. Were these really built in the memory of dead people? Or was there some other reason like pacifying the restless spirits of people who die in accidents. There was a real story to be discovered here. When I investigated further, I found so many tales that I was dumbstruck. The drivers who travelled on those roads had a different everyday experience. Here are those tales.

ɞ

'What rubbish! On Cart Road! Are you kidding? I just don't believe you,' stated Dheeraj, a bureaucrat. 'And the traffic is so heavy, there is no empty space, vehicles move one after the other in a snake-like queue all the time and you say there are ghosts haunting those roads? Funny!' he added.

He was right, but at night the situation was different, and some nights were more different than the others.

Anand narrated his experience which was totally in contrast from this objective analysis. A resident of Sanjauli, he was returning from Chandigarh after a meeting with his clients. He had started late from Chandigarh and it was

1.30 a.m. by the time he crossed the Shimla bus stand. Sleepy and tired, he was itching to reach home and get into his warm bed.

When he reached the Lift, he saw a lady. Her face was not visible but she had long hair and was wearing a sari. He was surprised to come across a woman all alone at this time of the night, but he did not want to stop. Who knew who she was—a tourist or a local of ill-repute perhaps. A few seconds after he'd passed her, he intuitively turned his head towards the right and saw a woman gliding alongside his car! It was the same lady. Shocked, he put his foot on the brake to stop the car. He got all muddled up. Did she want a lift or need help? Why was she running alongside the vehicle? But who can run so awkwardly like her, that too in a sari? He looked to his right again—there was no one there!

Now he was scared. He thought of getting out of the car to look for the woman, but changed his mind. He started the car again. He had reached the turn before the entrance to Hotel Holiday Home adjacent to the parking area when he saw the lady at the edge of the road, and he felt that something was definitely wrong. Somehow he knew that he would see her again and he was right. She was there, standing near the cliff just below the hotel on the blind curve a few metres ahead. It was an accident-prone site.

A bus had fallen there sometime back and a truck had also met the same fate. A couple of years ago a doctor had driven his vehicle straight into the ditch from there. A few metres before the bend, the lady was showing him the way and was guiding him to drive straight. He was aware that there was a curve to the left but today he saw a straight road ahead.

How could it be? He decided to take the left turn even though he couldn't see a road there! Just as he turned the steering to the left, the lady disappeared and so did the straight patch of road, and the curve came back. He was shell-shocked, but kept his cool. He slowly drove towards the left, praying fervently and thanking God for guiding him.

ထ

Four friends from Haryana stopped to have tea at a roadside dhaba in Kandyali, which is at a distance of seven kilometres from the famous resort of Narkanda. They were off to Spiti, an unexplored region of Himachal. It was 25 December, Christmas day, and they had planned to celebrate Christmas in Narkanda. It was 9 p.m. Just as they were paying for their tea, they heard loud music and a Bolero zipped past them at high speed. The occupants of the vehicle were singing raucously with beer bottles in their hands and two of them were, in fact, dangling out of the windows.

'Too bad, too bad, they are gone,' said the dhaba owner. The friends looked at him quizzically. The pahari owner then added, 'She is waiting for them at Firnu-mor.'

'What in hell is he saying?' one of the friends asked another.

The other shrugged and said, 'These paharis have their own language. Let us make a move, it is already very late.'

They reached Narkanda in another twenty minutes. They had a good Christmas dinner there. The next day they left for Spiti.

On their way back after enjoying four days in the desert in the coldest month, and surviving landslides and a snowstorm, they decided to break journey at Narkanda again. They wanted to spend New Year in Shimla and then drive off to Karnal.

At the hotel they were told about the accident that had happened the day they had come from Shimla. Since the vehicle had descended deep into the gorge no one came to know until the next morning. It was a miracle that the occupants, though seriously injured, survived. The friends recalled the Bolero they had seen that night with drunken occupants, as well as the strange statement of the dhabawallah. They asked the hotel manager what the shopkeeper meant and how he knew something bad would happen even before the accident took place. After a lot of persuasion they were told about 'her' and her reaction to drunkards!

A few decades ago, a husband and wife were travelling in a jeep to Narkanda. Their two children were at home in the village. The husband had had too many drinks. Despite the pleas of his wife to not drive but stay at their relatives' place, the husband did not budge. About one kilometre before Narkanda, at what is popularly known as Firnu-mor, he lost control of the jeep and it fell into the gorge.

The lady died, and now her spirit wanders around Firnu-mor. She attacks only drunkards, especially drivers, but she also haunts those who walk here in an inebriated state. She makes drunk drivers lose their concentration, scares them and leads them into the gorge. Thankfully though, no one is killed. In fact, the local people don't cross this area when they are drunk. No one wants to fall into the gorge!

The friends were stunned. One of them summed up their feelings, 'This is the right treatment for drunkards, they deserve it!'

ଊ

'Where am I?' mumbled Sita Ram, the bus driver.

'In the hospital,' the nurse said as she felt his pulse.

'What happened?' he asked her in a dazed state.

'That is what the police will ask you,' said the nurse sternly.

'I don't know, but the bus...' he murmured. 'How many died?' he asked tentatively.

'Eleven people. How did the bus go down the gorge on such a broad part of the road? Did you doze off?' asked the nurse accusingly.

'I...' he mumbled and then went quiet. He remembered that he was driving from Kingal to Baragaon, it was not very late, just 11 p.m. As he was about to turn the bus on one of the curves, he saw a lady with a child in her arms gesturing him to stop the bus. What was the lady doing so late in the night there on the deserted stretch, he thought and unknowingly followed the road. Before he realized there was no curve, where there should have been one, the bus tumbled down. And now he was here in the hospital. How would he explain this to the relatives of the deceased or, for that matter, to the police?

ଔ

The truck driver and his assistant were dead tired. It was the apple season, and it was their second trip out of Shimla. They were, in fact, forced to make the journey since a number of trucks were requisitioned by the government to transport the apple crop. After crossing Theog they decided to call it a day and stop at any wide patch of the road. It was already 2 a.m. They had been asked to report at Kotgarh, some 60 kilometres ahead of Theog.

When they crossed Matiana, a village on the National Highway, deserted at this time of the night, they decided to stop a few kilometres further down. They reached Nanni Dhank, and at an appropriate wide patch the driver stopped the truck and the conductor got down to wedge stones behind the rear tyres. Just as he was looking for the right-sized boulders, he heard some voices. Astonished that there were people around at this time in this desolate place, he called out to the driver and said that there was someone nearby.

By the time the driver got down from the truck, the conductor noticed a light flickering at a distance. Was it a house, or fire lit by someone, or a torch? The driver, a little irritated, demanded what the problem was, when he too heard people talking. They both stared at each other in astonishment and the conductor pointed towards the light, it was flickering on and off.

'What are you getting so scared of? Have some courage, these are just people. Come let us check on them,' the driver said.

'People? At this hour?' mumbled the conductor and shook his head, 'I am not going. You go and check.'

The driver walked off angry with the conductor. It was already so late, they should be sleeping instead of wandering around talking to people. There was a lot of work to be done the next day.

A few moments later the conductor heard someone running and then heard the driver's petrified voice, 'Get inside the truck, get inside the truck.' The conductor jumped in too, panic-stricken to ask for reasons.

The driver drove away from that area quickly and stopped only when he reached the Apple Check Post, some kilometres ahead. He told the conductor that when he reached the source of light, he saw no one but heard voices. Surprised, he looked around, but there was no one there. And then the voices stopped too, there was just silence and he felt something crawling on him, all slithery and creepy. He got so frightened that he ran towards the truck.

It was at the check post that they got to know from other drivers that, at that very spot, two buses along with their passengers got buried in a landslide a few decades ago and many people had heard voices and seen light there afterwards.

ଓ

Devi Mor—a stretch of about two kilometres between Theog and Sandhu on the National Highway, where a temple stands—is one of the most well-known haunted roads of the area. Earlier, when there were no roads and people travelled on foot or on mules, many a time they were accompanied by a white ghost who escorted them till a particular spot.

It was said that if you let it walk beside you, did not look at *it* and did not show your fear, it would not bother you. Those who followed the rules were let off by the ghost with the words, '*Aaj maine tujhe chor diya…tu bach gaya.*' And those who didn't, had to face the wrath of the ghost.

Different versions of the story about this ghost are in circulation. Some say, it is 'Fand Ka', while others say it is Bansheera. Some others say it is the spirit of Pantha, a man who died in snow (the place is also known as Pantha, in the memory of the same man). A lot of accidents happen on this patch. The story of this haunted spot has found its way into a folk song which describes how the ghost walks besides travellers.

ʚ

The couple boarded an HRTC bus from Chandigarh to Shimla on a winter night. After Solan they were only two passengers apart from the driver and conductor. The bus had just crossed Kandaghat, 15 kilometres ahead of Solan, when the following conversation began:

'Now we have come to the tricky part,' said the conductor.

'Why?' the driver asked.

'This is the stretch where you meet "the family" near the road. A woman, a man and a child on a scooter,' he said softly.

'*Arre chup reh*, they may be a family going somewhere in emergency?' the driver replied brushing it off.

'How can they be standing at the same spot in the same position whenever they are spotted?' asked the conductor. 'You remember what happened to the driver two weeks back?' he added.

'The Chandigarh–Rampur one?'

'Yes, actually he got scared, but thank God another bus came from the direction of Shimla at the same time, otherwise who knows what would have happened?' said the conductor.

'So, bhaiya, the rule is to ignore them. Don't stop. No need to pick anyone up,' the conductor added firmly.

'Achha, I get it,' said the driver.

Were they serious? The couple looked at each other with bewilderment.

And then the conductor said, 'We have crossed that spot. Nothing to worry now. They are not standing here today.'

'*Maine nahin darna tha*. Anyway, I would not have stopped the bus. I am not a fool.' The driver retorted laughingly.

The couple sighed in relief.

Acknowledgements

I am thankful to my family for their love and patience, affection and understanding, especially my parents-in-law, Swarn Lata and B S Kanwar; and my parents, Tripta Devi and J R Chaudhry. This book would not have been possible without the constructive criticism of Rakesh, my soulmate.

A special thanks to my friends—Ajay Goel, Hemlata and Rakesh Kainthla—who read through the manuscript meticulously and suggested changes. Their inputs and suggestions were invaluable.

I am grateful to my young friends—Aakriti, Aashish, Aayushi, Aashu, Abhishek, Abhinav, Abhilasha, Adya, Akshita, Akshta, Akshti, Ambar, Ankur, Anubhav, Ankur, Anne, Bhanvi, Chandni, Cheekoo, Deepika, Dhruv, Garima, Gorky, Gunjan, Himani, Kanishk, Keshav, Komal, Madhav,

Mayank, Mehak, Mallvi, Manyata, Nanha, Niharika, Namya, Parth, Pragandh, Prajwal, Pushpanjali, Riya, Rose, Shubhrattan, Sidharth, Swastik, Shilpa, Shaheen, Sunaina, Shruti, Shrey, Sonal, Smriti, Shubham, Vaivabh, Vardaan, Varun, Vasundhara, Vyom. Akarshan, Priyanka and many others for their persistent reminders for the second volume of ghost stories.

I also thank Professor Vepa Rao for supporting and guiding me in all my writing projects. Special thanks are due to the editorial team at Rupa Publications, especially my editor, Aishwarya Iyer, who helped edit and tighten the stories. I also thank my publishers, R K Mehra and Kapish Mehra, for their constant encouragement and support.